TRAIL OF REVENGE

W⊦ ⬚ the body of Kathy Rockhill is found in ⬚ck Hawksley's hotel room in Red S ⬚ s he is arrested on a murder charge. T ⬚ two families are thrown into conflict ar ⬚ an McCoy, the sheriff of Red Springs, h⬚ ⬚ough time keeping them apart. How D ⬚ides the trail of revenge makes a g ⬚ g yarn of gun-smoke and hot lead.

TRAIL OF REVENGE

TRAIL OF REVENGE

by

Jim Bowden

Dales Large Print Books
Long Preston, North Yorkshire,
BD23 4ND, England.

British Library Cataloguing in Publication Data.

Bowden, Jim
    Trail of revenge.

    A catalogue record of this book is
    available from the British Library

    ISBN   978-1-84262-702-0 pbk

First published in Great Britain in 1964 by Robert Hale Ltd.

Published in Large Print 2010 by arrangement with
Mr W. D. Spence

Dales Large Print is an imprint of Library Magna Books Ltd.

Printed and bound in Great Britain by
T.J. (International) Ltd., Cornwall, PL28 8RW

Chapter One

'You know I'm not a man to mince words, Pete, so I'll come straight to the point.' Al Rockhill looked hard at his friend as he stepped on to the verandah of the Broken K ranch-house. 'I think it's time you talked a bit of sense into Mick, got him to settle down and cut out his wild ways.'

Pete Hawksley laughed. 'You've hardly got off your horse than you're at me. Come on in and hev a drink.' He saw the deep concern in Al's grey eyes and the serious expression on his friend's face halted his laugh. He patted Al on the shoulder. 'Don't take it too seriously,' he added, leading Al into the house.

They crossed the hallway and entered a large room where Al Rockhill waited silently as he watched Pete Hawksley pour out two glasses of whisky. He saw a tall, powerfully built man of fifty, handsome, his dark hair greying at the temples.

Pete handed a glass to his friend. 'Sit down,' he said, 'We'll talk this thing over.'

He watched Rockhill closely as Al lowered himself into a chair. He was a big man; broad frame which at the age of fifty-three was beginning to fill out rather more than he liked. A powerful pair of shoulders ran into a thick neck so that his head seemed to be set upon the shoulders.

Rockhill sipped his whisky. 'It's no good treating this thing lightly, Pete,' he said. 'You know as well as I do the reputation Mick has, an' if your son's goin' to marry my daughter then I reckon it's time he settled down.'

Pete smiled, 'Don't take all these stories seriously,' he replied. 'I'll admit he has been a bit wild but these things tend to get exaggerated, besides he's not as bad as he was.'

'That may be,' answered Al, 'but all the same I reckon you should hev a word with him.'

'If it will ease your mind,' replied Pete, 'I'll do that. You know, Al, we've both come a long way since you bought the Twisted M an' I know it's dear to both our hearts to see the two spreads united through Kathy and Mick.'

Al nodded. 'I should hate to see anything spoil that,' he said. 'You could hev had the Twisted M when it came up for sale five years ago an' I'll be ever grateful to you for steppin' down and lettin' me, a newcomer seekin' a home, hev it.'

'Think nothin' of it,' said Pete, 'an' nothin' is going to spoil the unification of the two spreads.' A gleam came into his eye. 'It will be the most powerful cattle empire north of Red Springs.'

'It won't be if Mick doesn't settle down,' said Rockhill. 'I don't like these visits he keeps makin' to Quanah.'

Pete laughed. 'We're both men of the world, aren't we, Al, let the boy have his fling, better now than when he's married.'

'That's not the point,' returned Al. 'I reckon it's time they were gettin' married, after all they're both twenty-three. What's holding them back?'

'I don't know,' replied Pete. 'It'll all come in its own good time.'

'Wal, I know Kathy will say yes whenever Mick puts the question. You know Kathy's been all my life since Martha died. There's nothin' I wouldn't do for her. I don't want to see her get hurt. To be quite frank with you, you an' Betty have spoiled Mick.' He saw his friend stiffen and hastened to add, 'I think a lot about him, don't get the wrong idea.'

Pete smiled at Al's serious face. 'Stop worryin', Al, I'll make sure it's all right. I'll have a word with Mick when he gets back from Red Springs: he's spending a couple of days there putting through a big cattle deal for me; thought I'd better let him git used to handlin' these things.'

'Kathy told me about it and said she wouldn't be seein' Mick for a couple of days,' said Al. He paused thoughtfully then added. 'I hope that's all he is doin' in Red Springs.'

Pete smiled. 'Don't worry, old friend, everything will turn out all right.'

Kathy Rockhill kept her horse to a steady pace as she rode near the southern extremity of her father's ranch. A pretty girl, fair-haired, she had ridden for most of the afternoon lost in her thoughts; her mind had drifted to the past and she was thankful that five years ago they had been able to start a new life in the Brazos area of Texas. The years spent in Gainesville had become a faded memory in the happiness she had found on the Twisted M. She realized her father owed a lot to Pete Hawksley and she knew of their hopes for a big cattle empire through her marriage with Mick Hawksley. She sighed contentedly; she loved Mick very much but she wondered why he had not put the question of marriage to her.

Suddenly she pulled her horse to a halt realizing that it was late in the afternoon and she should be returning home very soon. Glancing round she saw that she had ridden further than she thought and was close to Broken K land and near a little wooded valley in which she and Mick had spent many pleasant hours. She pushed her horse forward and in a few minutes was on the edge of the valley. Dismounting, she led the animal forward, tied it to the nearest tree, walked further down the slope and sat down under a tree. She glanced through the trees to a little stream which flowed along the bottom of the valley, wishing that Mick was with her now.

Suddenly she was startled by a peal of laughter. She sat upright, glanced round but could see no one. The laughter rang through the wood again and Kathy scrambled to her feet but quickly stepped behind a tree when she saw a girl of about her own age running alongside the stream. Suddenly she gasped, her whole body stiffened when she saw a man scramble to his feet and run after the girl.

'Mick!' Kathy did not know the word had escaped her lips. Her eyes widened with shock and her face drained of its colour.

The girl kept half turning as she ran, her laughter echoing round the valley. Mick Hawksley gained on her then, catching her round the waist, stopped her. The girl struggled until Mick's lips touched hers then she relaxed in his arms. When their lips parted they both turned and with their arms round each others waist walked along the valley and were lost amongst the trees.

Kathy stared disbelievingly at the spot where they had stood. Her whole body was petrified with shock; her hands were clenched so tightly that her nails dug deep into her palms. A sudden burst of laughter jerked her back to reality. She sank against the tree, her hand coming to her mouth as she sobbed and fought to keep back her tears.

'Mick with a saloon girl in our valley!' she whispered half to herself as if she had to voice the words in order to believe what she had seen.

She straightened and pushed herself from the tree, tempted to reveal herself, but, instead, she moved forward a few paces until she had them in sight again. They were still walking beside the stream but a moment later they turned up the hillside and Kathy's attention was drawn to a buggy which stood at the top of the rise on the opposite side of the valley. She watched them reach the buggy and after Mick had helped the girl into the seat he climbed up beside her, flicked the reins and turned the horse in the direction of Red Springs.

When they had passed from view Kathy scrambled up the hillside to her horse. The horror of seeing Mick with another girl now turned to fury and she was shaking with pent up temper as she climbed into the saddle. She put her horse down the hillside guiding it skilfully through the trees, splashed across the brook and urged the animal up the opposite slope. When she broke from the trees and topped the rise she saw that the buggy was moving at a brisk pace across the undulating grassland. Kathy hesitated a moment then sent her horse after the buggy taking care to hang far enough back so that she would not attract the attention of its occupants.

So intent was she on watching the buggy that she failed to notice a horseman some distance to the east on Broken K land check his horse, watch the progress of the two parties for a few minutes, then turn his horse and ride in the same direction matching his pace to theirs.

Chapter Two

The light was fading from the sky when Red Springs came in sight. All thought of returning to the Twisted M had gone from Kathy's mind; she felt she must see Mick and have this thing out with him once and for all.

Kathy hung back when they reached the town and halted her horse a short distance along the main street. She saw Mick drive the buggy to the Silver Dollar. The girl jumped down from the seat, smiled at Mick then hurried into the saloon. Mick turned the buggy and drove quickly to the livery stable. He reappeared a few moments later and walked quickly to the hotel. When he disappeared into the building Kathy walked her horse forward, slipped from the saddle in front of the hotel, tied her horse to the rail and hurried inside.

Almost at the same moment a cowboy swung from his horse a short distance along the street and, after securing it, strolled along the sidewalk until he was a few yards from the hotel doorway. He leaned against the wall in the shadows, rolled himself a cigarette and waited.

When Kathy entered the hotel there was only the clerk behind the desk in the lobby. He looked surprised when he saw her.

'Good evening, Miss Kathy,' he said. 'Not very often we see you here at this time of day.'

'I believe I saw Mick Hawksley come in here,' she said. 'I'd like to see him.'

'Certainly,' replied the clerk. 'You'll find him in room ten.'

'Thanks,' answered the girl who spun on her heel and hurried up the stairs.

She tapped lightly on the door of room ten and it was opened almost immediately by the young man.

'Kathy!' gasped Mick. 'What on earth are you doing here?'

Kathy did not answer but her look, as she brushed past him into the room, cut deep into Mick. He shut the door and turned looking at her with a mixture of surprise and curiosity showing on his face.

She spun round to face him, her face black with anger. All the fury she had felt back on the prairie suddenly released itself in a torrent of words which were flung from her lips.

'I saw you today,' she cried, 'carrying on

16

with a saloon girl, out there on your father's land in the little valley; our valley we'd called it. Remember, Mick, we used to go there. Now you bring this … this … no good hussy there. How much patience have I got to have, Mick? I thought you were settling down and some of the wildness of three or four years ago had gone for ever. Now I see you carrying on on your own doorstep. I thought you were supposed to be in town putting through a deal for your father.' Kathy's face had gone white with fury, her eyes stared wildly at Mick.

Mick was taken by surprise at the sudden outburst. He stared almost unbelievingly at the girl for a moment then, realizing it was no use denying his actions he bit his lip, stepped towards the girl but she turned away.

'Kathy,' he said, his voice soft. 'I'm sorry but there's nothing in it really.'

'Nothing in it?' Kathy tossed her head haughtily in shocked surprise. 'I saw you, remember, those kisses…'

'Were not serious,' put in Mick sharply. 'I have been in Red Springs on business for my father, I put through a big deal for cattle at better terms than I expected; I felt like celebrating.'

'Funny way to celebrate,' snapped Kathy.

'I had a few drinks,' went on Mick, 'then felt like a ride in the country, the girl was free so I took her with me.'

'Why couldn't you have driven home instead?' asked Kathy sharply.

'Dad wasn't expecting me home until to-morrow so I thought I'd make of the chance to see some of the boys in town tonight.'

'Boys?' scoffed Kathy.

'Believe me there was nothing more to it than what you saw today,' replied Mick.

'Maybe, but I'm not prepared to be played around with,' said Kathy hotly. 'We're supposed to be getting married but I don't want to be the laughing stock of the neighbour-hood.'

Mick's face became very serious. 'Kathy,' he said, 'I think an awful lot about you but I haven't asked you to marry me.' Words sprung to the girl's lips but Mick went on quickly halting them before they were spoken. 'I know everyone expects us to marry; our parents look upon it as settled; the whole countryside thinks it's the right thing, but I'm not sure I love you.'

Kathy stared at Mick. 'I love you very much,' she whispered. 'I thought you...' Her voice trailed away, tears coming to her eyes.

18

'I don't want to hurt you, Kathy,' said Mick, 'and that's why I want to be certain before I ask you.'

The girl looked up suddenly, her eyes blazing. 'You'll never be certain,' she said, 'so long as you're running around with saloon girls. Don't you think that hurts me? And what about your trips to Quanah? You don't expect…'

'There's been many rumours about my visits to Quanah,' cut in Mick hotly. 'If you've cared to believe them then that's your business but I'll tell you now that apart from my first two visits those rumours are wrong.'

'Then why have you been going there so much lately?' asked Kathy. 'What I've seen today seems to add proof to what I've heard.'

'Once a person gets a bad name it sticks,' replied Mick, 'and much that never happens is put at that person's door.' He paused thoughtfully then looked hard at the girl in front of him. 'Kathy,' he said, 'I'm going to tell you something which I did not intend telling anyone for some time. I have been visiting Quanah to help a girl.' Kathy stared curiously at him but waited for him to explain. 'You know I would prefer my father to let me manage the ranch more than he does – this is the first big deal he's let me put

19

through and most of that was cut and dried. Well, I've been wanting the opportunity to prove that I was capable of handling things. On one of my visits to Quanah I met this girl; her father and mother had just been killed in a buggy accident, they were ranchers and she was left with the whole spread to run. She had a good foreman and a good set of punchers but she needed some guidance on the paper work, the financial side, and the management of the whole thing. I saw an opportunity of proving my capabilities to dad so I offered to help her and that has been the reason for my frequent visits to Quanah.'

'Why didn't you tell your father this?' said Kathy.

'It wouldn't have been any use,' explained Mick. 'He'd have stepped in and done the job. Don't you see, Kathy, it would have been the same treatment as I've been getting on the Broken K. I wanted to do this job myself to prove I could run a ranch. I would have told him when the ranch was running successfully.'

Kathy understood Mick's feelings. 'But why didn't you tell me?' she asked. 'Couldn't you trust me to keep your secret?'

'Yes I could,' replied Mick, 'but there was

a girl involved and I thought you might be jealous and in that jealousy tell my father.'

A thought suddenly struck Kathy; a doubt entered her mind. 'I suppose she's pretty,' she said scornfully.

'Yes she is,' replied Mick, not liking Kathy's tone.

'Then maybe it's her whom you love,' lashed Kathy viciously.

'Maybe,' snapped Mick. 'If that's what you want to believe. It's just as I thought, you are jealous, thank goodness I didn't tell you.'

'But I know now, don't I?' smiled Kathy meaningly.

'You wouldn't...' gasped Mick. 'If you do I'll...'

'Then settle down, Mick, and marry me,' snapped Kathy.

'I've told you I don't know whether I love you or not,' answered Mick. 'Don't you see I'm thinking of you.'

'You're impossible,' snapped Kathy irately. She turned to the door, flung it open and stormed out slamming the door behind her.

Mick stared at the door angrily for a moment, cursed under his breath, crossed to the window and stood looking out for a few minutes as his brain pounded through the stormy scene with Kathy. Suddenly he spun round, grabbed his Stetson from a chair and hurried from the room. He took the stairs two at a time, stormed past the surprised clerk, left the hotel and hurried along the sidewalk in the direction of the Silver Dollar.

A cowboy straightened in the shadows and watched Mick Hawksley. A faint smile of satisfaction flicked his lips. 'Both in a temper,' he muttered. 'Maybe the chance I want is coming.' He leaned back against the wall and stared in the direction of the café on the other side of the street.

When Kathy left the hotel she snatched the horse's reins from the rail, reached for the saddle then stopped. Her thoughts raced. 'Why should I give up so easily,' she whispered to herself. 'I'll give him time to simmer down.' She led the horse across the street, tied it to a rail and entered the café. Almost three-quarters of an hour passed before Kathy emerged into the darkness of Red Springs. She glanced along the street and hurried across the road to the hotel.

A cowboy, his thoughts racing, watched her. Why was she returning to the hotel? They had both left separately, in tempers, so what was she up to? As Kathy reached the door he straightened and, when she disappeared inside, he hurried forward. Glancing through the lobby window he saw Kathy approaching the clerk who was behind his desk. The cowboy moved swiftly to the door and easing it slightly open he inclined his head to listen.

'Is Mick still in?' asked Kathy.

'No,' replied the clerk. 'He went out shortly after you had left.'

'But I must see him.' There was an urgent, almost desperate, tone in Kathy's voice. 'Do you know where he went?'

'No,' answered the clerk.

'Then I'll wait in room ten,' said Kathy. 'I must see him you see, I'm going to marry him.'

The man at the door stiffened. His face darkened with anger and frustration. He turned from the door, his brain pounding. He banged his fist and palm together, annoyed at a turn of events he had not expected. 'They'd obviously had a row,' he muttered to himself. 'Now this; what the…' Suddenly he swung on his heel and hurried along the sidewalk towards the Silver Dollar determined to keep his eye on Mick Hawksley and see what turned up.

He pushed his way through the doorway into the saloon. The huge room was crowded; in one section the gambling tables were surrounded by customers and all the tables covering the rest of the floor were occupied whilst at the long mahogany counter cowboys from neighbouring ranches mingled with townsfolk clamouring for drinks. As he weaved his way between tables towards the bar the man saw Mick Hawksley seated at a table near the stage, a bottle of whisky in front of him. The cowboy reached the bar, called for a drink and took up a position from which he could keep Hawksley under observation.

Mick stared morosely at the bottle, picked up his glass, drained it and poured himself another drink. Four glasses of whisky had been drunk when a saloon girl moved up behind him, took off his Stetson and dropped it on the table. She slid her arms over his shoulders, bent down and kissed him lightly on the side of the head before swinging round and sitting on a chair beside him.

'Thanks for this afternoon, Mick,' she smiled.

'That's all right, Laura,' he replied casually, his face expressionless.

The girl was taken aback at his off-hand manner and the smile was replaced by a mixed look of concern and hurt. 'What's wrong, Mick?' she asked. 'Didn't you enjoy it?'

'Sure, sure,' answered Mick and drained his glass.

'Then why are you like this?' she said. 'There could be a lot more like it, and better if you wanted it.'

Mick stared at his glass as if he had not heard her. He grabbed the bottle and poured another drink.

Laura's eyes clouded with anger. She grabbed his arm. 'Did you hear what I said?' she snapped.

Mick shook her hand off. 'Shut up,' he snarled. 'Leave me alone, I want to think.'

The girl's eyes blazed into fury. 'Don't be so high and mighty,' she shouted. 'You don't order me around like that and get away with it; it was a different story this afternoon. I suppose it's your precious Kathy Rockhill you're thinking about!' People turned to stare at the saloon girl who had jumped to her feet and was staring angrily at the man at the table. He ignored her and drank his whisky. This infuriated her all the more. 'Don't come running back to me if this goes sour on you!' she screamed. She tossed her head back haughtily and hurried to the bar where other admirers soon bought her a drink. The silence which had descended on the saloon was quickly replaced by the usual din and the incident was forgotten in all but a few minds.

Mick Hawksley drank steadily throughout the evening and when, at about ten o'clock, he decided to go and pushed himself to his feet he swayed and gripped the table for support. He stood for a few moments, picked up his Stetson and then weaved his way unsteadily between the tables to the door.

A cowboy at the bar finished his drink quickly and hurried out of the Silver Dollar. He paused on the sidewalk and watched Mick Hawksley swaying unsteadily, supporting himself every now and then either on the rail or the wall of the adjacent buildings. The man turned and followed slowly.

About two hundred yards along the street the continuation of the sidewalk was broken by an alley. Mick paused at the steps at the end of the sidewalk then tottered down them, lost his balance and staggered into the alley. The man glanced round and, seeing no one in sight, hurried forward and turned into the darkness of the alley. He had taken about five paces when his foot caught something and he almost fell. Bending down he saw it was the unconscious form of Mick Hawksley.

'Passed out cold,' the man grinned to

himself. He quickly ran his hands through Mick's pockets and finding a wallet transferred it to his own back pocket. Finding a knife in Mick's belt he held it thoughtfully. 'This is better than I thought,' he muttered. 'Now to surprise Kathy.' He pushed the knife through his own belt, found Mick's Stetson and dragged him to his feet. Slinging the unconscious man over his shoulder he made his way carefully along the alley and turned along a back street to reach the back door of the hotel. He was thankful that there was no one about and testing the door was relieved to find it unlocked. He pushed it open gently and stepped into a dimly lit corridor.

He could hear the clerk at the far end talking to someone in the lobby. He edged his way forward carefully to the back stairs which he mounted quickly but silently and had soon reached room ten without being seen. After tapping lightly on the door he had to wait only a moment before it was opened.

Kathy gasped; her eyes widened with surprise and concern when she saw Mick's unconscious form across the man's shoulder. 'What's happened?' she asked, stepping to one side to allow the man to pass.

The cowboy crossed to the bed, tipped Hawksley on to it and turned to face Kathy who had closed the door.

'He's been drinkin' heavily in the Silver Dollar,' he explained. 'I followed him when he left. He passed out in an alley so I brought him back here.'

'That's kind of you,' she said. 'May I ask you one more favour? Please don't tell his father.'

The man nodded. 'Sure, Kathy,' he said. He smiled to himself when he saw the surprised look on her face.

Kathy was puzzled and a little annoyed for this man had not used her Christian name before.

'I won't say a word,' he went on, 'because he'll hev a bigger mystery on his hands.'

'What do you mean?' asked Kathy puzzled by his remark.

'You don't really remember me do you, Kathy?' replied the cowboy. 'Oh you know me, but I've altered a lot in five, tough years an' you've never recognized me as the kid you snubbed when he was eighteen!'

Kathy gasped. Her thoughts raced back over the years. 'Gainesville!' Her voice was scarcely above a whisper. She stared at the cowboy who grinned at her. Slowly recog-

28

nition came to her mind and her eyes widened with horror. 'You!' The word hissed from between her tight lips. 'No! Not you.'

She leaped for the door but the man was quicker. He grasped her round the waist with one arm and as she opened her mouth to scream he clasped his other hand over it. Terror was in her eyes as she stared up into the dark face which grinned evilly down at her. Slowly the man eased her back towards the bed.

'I've waited years for revenge on you and your father,' he hissed. 'I was prepared to forget it when I was foolish enough to think there might still be a hope with you. I knew you were sweet on Hawksley an' tonight I heard you say you were going to marry him.' His eyes full of hate narrowed with the thought. He forced Kathy back across the foot of the bed pressing her head down with brutal force. Drawing Hawksley's knife from his belt he grinned at the terror stricken girl who struggled unsuccessfully to get free. 'This will hit your father as well, an' there's more to come for him, an' Hawksley will get the blame.' The blade flashed as he plunged it downwards with such force that it buried itself to the hilt in Kathy's body.

For a moment the cowboy stared at the

lifeless body of the girl then straightened slowly. Suddenly he turned and went to the door but with his hand on the knob he hesitated. He glanced round the room and when he was sure there was nothing to betray his visit he opened the door slowly. Making sure there was no one in the corridor he stepped out of the room, closed the door and had soon left the hotel by the back door to disappear into the night.

Chapter Three

The clerk in the hotel lobby pulled a watch from his waistcoat pocket and glanced at it nervously. It was getting late and he was worried because Kathy Rockhill was having such a long wait for Mick Hawksley. He went to the door, stepped on to the sidewalk and looked up and down the street but no one was heading for the hotel. He waited a moment half hoping that Hawksley would appear but no one left the Silver Dollar. Making up his mind to have a word with Kathy he re-entered the hotel and made his way to room ten.

A puzzled frown creased his forehead when he received no answer after tapping lightly on the door. His second knock almost remained unanswered and finding the door unlocked he pushed it open slowly, almost apologetically for his intrusion. Suddenly he stiffened with horror at the scene before him. Kathy Rockhill, a knife buried deep in her body sprawled across the foot of the bed and Mick Hawksley was standing, staring stupidly at the girl.

'Mister Hawksley, what's happened?' asked the clerk.

Mick turned round slowly, then sat down on the side of the bed burying his head in his hands. His head throbbed as if a thousand hammers were beating inside it. The clerk stepped into the room and repeated his question.

Mick raised his head slowly, staring at the clerk as if it was the first time he was aware of his presence. 'Charlie,' he slurred, 'I don't...' He pushed himself to his feet, staggered and had to grasp the bed head for support.

'You'd better wait here, Mister Hawksley,' said the clerk, suddenly galvanized into action when the full seriousness of the situation hit him. 'I'll get some help.' He turned and hurried from the room shutting the door behind him. He fumbled in his pocket for a master-key and locked the door before hurrying down the stairs and out into the street.

Thankful to see a light still burning in the sheriff's office he ran across the street and flung open the door. The four occupants of the room looked round startled by the suddenness of the intrusion. Dan McCoy, the tall, lean, tough Sheriff of Red Springs, stared at the clerk standing in the middle of the office panting for breath.

'What's matter, Charlie, you look as if you've seen a ghost?' he said.

'Worse than that,' gasped the clerk. 'Mick Hawksley's murdered Kathy Rockhill in the hotel!'

'What!' the sheriff jumped to his feet, his long slim fingers reaching for his Stetson. There was a glint in his steel-blue eyes which bore ill-will for the murderer, especially the murderer of a woman.

The other three men were on their feet with him. A grim look clouded the weather-beaten, leather face of the fifty-three year old deputy-sheriff, Clint Schofield. He liked Mick Hawksley and could not see him as the murderer of the girl everyone expected him to marry. Jack and Howard Collins, Dan's brothers-in-law were close on his heels when he strode from the office. They ran across the street and Charlie led the way to Hawksley's room.

'I locked it,' he panted as he inserted the key in the lock. 'Thought it best.' He threw the door open and stood back to allow the sheriff to enter.

Dan glanced at the body on the bed then at Mick who stood by the open window breathing deeply trying to clear his head with the cool night air. He turned when he heard the door open and leaned against the sill staring at the five men.

'Mick, what's happened?' rapped Dan. Hawksley shook his head slowly. 'I remember leaving the Silver Dollar, after that nothing until I woke up here with Kathy's body across the foot of the bed.' The effects of the drink coupled with the shock and the presence of the lawman suddenly reacted on the young man. He leaned limply against the wall, his face twisted as if he were trying to probe the depths of his mind for some clue to the blank time. His body started shaking, 'I didn't do it, I'll swear I didn't,' he sobbed between tight lips.

Dan scowled, crossed the room and gripped the young man by the arm. 'Pull yourself together, Hawksley,' he snapped. 'You're in a bad enough jam as it is without crackin' up.' He led Mick towards the body. 'Is that your knife?' he asked.

Words choked in Mick's throat as he looked down at the girl. He nodded.

Dan turned to Clint. 'You'd better take him back to the office. I'll talk to him over there.'

Clint nodded and escorted Mick from the room.

'This is a bad job,' went on Dan turning to the Collins brothers. 'The parents will have to be told an' it's no use delaying matters. I know you were about to leave for home but I'd be mighty grateful if one of you would ride to the Broken K an' the other to the Twisted M an' bring Al Rockhill an' Pete Hawksley back here.'

'Sure, Dan,' said Jack and the two brothers left the hotel, hurried to their horses, climbed into the saddles and left Red Springs by the north road on their grim errand.

When the Collins brothers had left room ten Dan closed the window, glanced round the room and, when he stepped into the corridor, instructed the clerk to lock the door.

The sheriff was very thoughtful as he walked down the stairs followed by the clerk. When they reached the lobby the clerk moved behind the counter and stood there watching Dan who was preoccupied with his thoughts. He saw a tall, slim, but powerfully built man of twenty-five whose clean-cut, weather-beaten face spoke of much time spent in the open.

Dan turned and looked at the clerk. 'Charlie,' he said, 'when you came for me you said Mick had murdered Kathy; what made you so sure?'

'Well he was there in the room and she was dead,' replied Charlie.

'But that's no proof that he did it,' pointed out Dan.

'I saw…' began the clerk.

'Are you sure you saw anything?' cut in Dan. 'Think carefully before you speak an' be sure it's not what you thought happened.' Dan knew Charlie's capacity for romancing and putting his own interpretation on things.

'Well,' replied Charlie rather sheepishly, 'I guess when I think of it I saw nothing except Mick in that room and the body on the bed.'

'Then you can't swear positively that Mick killed Kathy?' said Dan.

The clerk shook his head. 'No,' he answered quietly.

'Be careful what you say in future, Charlie,' advised Dan. 'I'll be back later an' I'll want to hear what you know about tonight, so sort things out in your mind correctly, an' don't let anyone in that room. I'll be sending Clint over to see to things.'

Dan left the hotel and crossed the dusty street to his office. He found that Clint had locked Mick Hawksley in one of the cells. The young man was sitting on the wooden bunk and, with his elbows resting on his knees, held his head between his hands.

When the sheriff went back into his office he found Clint brewing some coffee on the stove.

'Thought he might like some black,' said Clint nodding towards the cells. His face was grim. 'Think he did it, Dan?'

'Looks bad for him,' replied Dan. 'Found with the body, an' his knife.'

'But Mick's not the type,' protested Clint.

'He was drunk an' there's no accountin' for what a person does in that state,' said Dan. 'However, there are a few things need checking. I'd like you to contact the doc an' the undertaker an' see to all the tidying up but first hev a look round that room, see if there's anything that might help us.'

Clint Schofield nodded, picked up his Stetson and left the office. When the coffee was ready the sheriff poured out a mug-full and entered Mick's cell.

'Drink this, Mick, then maybe you'll feel like trying to remember,' said Dan.

The young man took the mug gratefully and sipped at the black coffee. Dan waited until he had drunk half of it before he spoke.

'Feel like talkin' about it?' he asked.

'Guess so,' replied Mick. 'Got to sooner or later.' He paused looking thoughtful. 'If only I could remember,' he said sadly. There was a tone in his voice in which Dan recognized that Mick was reproaching himself for the death of Kathy whether he had actually plunged the knife or not.

'We'll try and piece things together,' said Dan quietly, trying to instill some confidence into Mick. 'You've been in town a few days,' went on Dan. 'When did Kathy arrive?'

'Early this evening,' replied Mick.

'And you saw her?' asked Dan.

'Sure,' said Mick. 'She followed me to the hotel and...' He stopped, wishing he had used different words.

Dan seized on them. 'What do you mean, followed?' he asked. Hawksley hesitated. 'It will be better for you if you tell me everything,' pressed Dan.

Mick shrugged his shoulders resignedly. 'I expect it will all come out,' he muttered. He went on to tell Dan of his trip with Laura and how Kathy had followed them and confronted him in the hotel.

'If anybody heard that argument,' said Dan, 'then things are really stacked against you; it provides a motive, drunk or not.'

'But Kathy left the hotel before me,' protested Mick.

'Then she must have returned,' said Dan thoughtfully. 'I wonder why? What happened after Kathy left?'

Mick went on to tell of his visit to the Silver Dollar. 'I'll admit I had every intention of getting drunk, an' I remember nothing after leaving the Silver Dollar until I came round in my room.'

'Did you see Laura again?' asked Dan.

'Sure,' replied Mick, 'but I gave her the brush-off.'

'Guess she wouldn't like that,' observed Dan wryly.

'Sure didn't,' said Mick. 'Made some sort of threat,' he added.

Dan made no comment but made a mental note of Mick's observation. Suddenly he switched the line of questioning. 'What have you been doing in town these last few days?' he asked.

'Putting through a cattle deal for my father,' answered Mick. 'I was successful an' was returning home tomorrow.' Suddenly he sat upright and hastily felt through his pockets, alarm showing on his face.

'What's wrong?' asked Dan curiously.

'Pa asked me to draw a thousand dollars from the bank,' explained Mick, an anxious tone in his voice. 'I was going to leave early in the morning before the bank was open so I drew it out today. Had it in my wallet.'

'An' now that's gone,' said Dan.

Mick nodded glumly.

'Anybody see you with that money?' asked the sheriff.

'Guess maybe I had my wallet out to pay for drinks in the Silver Dollar,' replied Mick. 'I've got into a pretty bad mess, haven't I?' he added glumly.

Dan did not answer but stood looking thoughtfully at the young man. He had known Mick Hawksley a long time. There was no real malice in the dark, medium-built young man; he had been spoilt and had too much money which had resulted in him being somewhat wild in his way when he had been young but over the last two years he had begun to settle down although rumours still clung to the name of Mick Hawksley.

The sound of the outside door of his office being opened interrupted Dan's thoughts. He left the cell to find Clint Schofield had returned.

'Everythin' taken care of,' said the wrinkled-faced deputy. 'There doesn't seem to be anythin' in thet room to shed light on this case but I've hed Charlie lock it up again; thought you might want a look.'

'You didn't find a wallet?' asked Dan.

Clint shook his head. 'Nope,' he replied. 'Why a wallet?'

'Mick had one with a thousand dollars in it,' said Dan. 'He hasn't got it now!' Clint let out a long low whistle. 'And there are other things need looking into. Kathy had a row with Mick, left the hotel and apparently returned after he'd gone to the Silver Dollar. Also, a saloon girl made some sort of threat to him. I'm going to have a word with her. If Rockhill and Hawksley arrive before I'm back hold them here.'

Although the hour was late there was still a big crowd of people in the Silver Dollar when Dan entered the saloon. He soon sought out Laura and apologized to her male companion for the interruption.

'Did you threaten Mick Hawksley earlier tonight?' asked Dan, coming straight to the point after he had taken the saloon girl to one side.

The girl was a little taken aback by the question and surprise showed on her face as she answered. 'What's he done, come blabbing to the lawman for protection?' she said scornfully. 'Sure, he stood me up, made a fool of me and I told him not to be surprised if things went sour on him.'

'That's all you said?' said Dan.

The girl nodded. 'He needn't come round...'

'Did you see him with a wallet?' cut in Dan.

'Sure,' laughed the girl. 'What's he done, lost it?' The smile suddenly vanished from her face. She stiffened and looked annoyed. 'Here, what you trying to do accuse me of stealing it?'

'I didn't say he'd lost it,' replied Dan.

'You implied it,' snapped Laura, 'and I don't sink to things like that. Lots of people could have seen him with it when he paid for his drinks.'

'See anybody follow him out of here?' queried the sheriff.

'I wasn't paying any attention to him,' replied the girl, 'he wasn't worth it.'

Dan thanked her and crossed to the bar where he repeated his last question to the barman only to be told that people had been coming and going all night and he had not noticed.

The sheriff left the saloon and walked thoughtfully to the hotel where he obtained the key for room ten from the clerk. He looked round the room carefully but it revealed nothing. Dan was about to leave when something on the floor beside the bed attracted his attention. Dropping on one knee he picked up two small pieces of clay from the carpet and examined them carefully. When he reached the lobby he returned the key to Charlie.

'When was that room last cleaned out?' he asked.

'This morning,' replied the clerk puzzled by the question. 'They are all cleaned out every morning.'

'It's not been touched since then?' pressed Dan.

'No,' answered Charlie.

'Who's been in that room since it was cleaned?' asked Dan.

'Only Mick Hawksley and Kathy Rockhill to my knowledge until I came for you.'

'Could anyone have gone there without you knowing?'

'I guess so,' replied Charlie. 'I'm in here most of the time but it's possible.'

The sheriff went on to question Charlie about the happenings earlier in the evening but his answers only left Dan with more puzzles. Why had Kathy on her return to the hotel said she was going to marry Mick when only an hour before they had had an argument?

When Dan returned to his office he produced the two small pieces of clay which he had carefully preserved since finding them.

'What do you make of that?' he asked Clint.

The deputy examined the particles. 'Wal, with thet red tinge in them they've come from only one place around here – Pony Creek on the Broken K spread,' said Clint.

'That's exactly what I thought,' said Dan. He spun round and strode to the cells followed by a bewildered deputy.

'Those the boots you were wearing this afternoon?' asked Dan.

Hawksley looked surprised at the question. 'Yes,' he replied. 'I was in too much of a temper to clean them after Kathy left.'

'Pass them to me,' ordered Dan.

Mick did not question the sheriff's demand, and when he handed them through the bars Dan examined them carefully before passing them back to the prisoner.

'Were you in Pony Creek today?' asked Dan, watching Mick carefully.

'No,' replied Mick and from his look of bewilderment Dan knew he was telling the truth.

When the two lawmen had returned to the office Clint looked curiously at Dan.

'What was all that about?' he asked, rubbing his chin.

'I found that clay in Mick's room,' replied Dan. 'Charlie assures me that the room was cleaned this morning therefore that means the clay came there after that. As far as Charlie knows only Mick and Kathy entered that room except for us. Neither you nor I have been in Pony Creek today; Jack, Howard and Charlie have not been out of town; Mick hasn't been there so that leaves Kathy.'

Clint began to realize what Dan was getting at. 'Kathy hadn't been there,' he said excitedly. 'When I helped the undertaker I noticed her riding boots were dusty with a slight trace of soil but certainly no red tinted clay!'

'Then someone else was in that room!' exclaimed Dan.

'I said Mick couldn't hev done it,' said Clint.

'Hold hard,' warned Dan. 'We haven't proved that. To most people this would be a straightforward case but with what we've learned in the past few hours it looks a bit different to us, we might even get him off with insufficient evidence but I've a feeling the knife would weigh too heavily against our points. However, the fact that we can prove someone else was in that room makes someone a vital witness in this murder.'

'Or maybe even a murderer!' urged Clint.

'Maybe, but we can't be certain, it could still have been Mick,' said Dan. The sound of horses stopping outside his office caused Dan to put the clay inside the drawer of his desk. 'Not a word to anyone about this, Clint,' he said.

The door burst open and Pete Hawksley strode in followed by Jack Collins.

'What's all this nonsense?' boomed Hawksley. 'My boy arrested for murder of the girl he was goin' to marry!'

'I had to arrest him,' replied Dan calmly. 'Evidence was too great.'

'Rubbish,' snapped Hawksley. 'You've missed somethin'. Let me hev a word with the boy. I'll git to the bottom of it.'

Dan led the way to the cells and when Mick saw his father he pushed himself to his feet and crossed to the bars.

'Now, son,' said Pete, 'what's all this nonsense about?' Dan had been prepared for Hawksley to fly off the handle at his son but he detected a note of softness in the deep voice and realized the deep affection the father had for the son.

'I know nothing about it, pa,' said Mick. 'I can't remember a thing, but I know I didn't murder Kathy; surely if I'd done a thing like that I would remember it?'

'That's good enough for me,' said Hawksley. 'Don't worry I'll hev you out of here before long. McCoy, if he says he didn't do it then he didn't. Oh, I know all about it, Collins explained it to me as we rode in, I know it looked black for Mick an' you hed to arrest him but you aren't goin' to hold him.' He turned to walk into the office when Mick called.

'Dad, I completed the deal, you can send the hands to pick up the herd at Rosewell,' he said.

'Good,' replied his father. 'I'll fix things. Did you get the money I wanted?'

Mick glanced sharply at Dan. 'I got it today an' was goin' to return early in the morning knowing you'd want to get the hands away for that herd but...' He hesitated. 'I lost it.'

'Lost it?' gasped Hawksley.

'We think it may have been stolen,' put in Dan.

Hawksley gritted his teeth. 'Then you've more than a murderer to find,' he snapped and swung back into the office. Suddenly he spun round on Dan. 'Somebody saw him flashing that money in the Silver Dollar, followed him back to the hotel, knocked him out, stole the money, and was disturbed by Kathy an' had to kill her.'

Dan smiled. 'Sorry, Mister Hawksley,' he said, admiring the way the father was determined to prove his son's innocence, 'but that won't hold together. Kathy was in that room when Mick returned so why wasn't she heard to scream? Would the killer have had time to take Mick's knife from his belt without Kathy doing a thing, besides there's no mark of violence on Mick.'

'Then how do you account for the missing thousand dollars?' snapped Hawksley, annoyed that McCoy had so easily disposed of his theories.

'Mick could have dropped it,' replied Dan. 'He was drunk, you know; or if he passed out someone could easily have relieved him of it.'

Further conversation was cut short as the door burst open to admit a grim-faced, tight-lipped Al Rockhill followed by Howard Collins. He halted in his tracks when he saw Pete Hawksley.

'You scum!' he hissed but his words lashed round the room and hit deep into Hawksley's mind. Rockhill was blinded by rage, all reasoning had gone from his mind at the sight of Hawksley, all thoughts that this was the man who had been his friend had gone. He leaped forward tigerishly but Dan, who had seen the glint in his eye, moved quicker and stepped between the two men pushing the big, powerful Rockhill away. Jack and Howard leaped forward and grabbed him by the arms.

'Calm yourself!' snapped Dan.

'Calm yourself?' shouted Rockhill. 'How do you expect me to do that after what's happened? He's to blame as much as his son. I told him long ago to take the boy in hand an' not spoil him. He's been too easy goin'. Let the boy hev his fling he used to say. If he'd stopped him he wouldn't hev been drunk tonight an' this wouldn't hev happened.'

'There could be other explanations,' said Dan.

'Collins told me Mick was found in the room an' his knife hed been used; that's sufficient evidence fer me an' I guess it will be fer a lot of other people,' stormed Rockhill. 'We'll see a hangin' in Red Springs.' He paused; his eyes narrowed as he looked straight at Hawksley. Hate flamed in them. 'But it won't end there,' he went on. 'I'll see you suffer fer what's happened; my world has collapsed at the hands of your son an' you're as much to blame. I'll git even with you if it takes the rest of my life to do it!'

Pete's face had gone white under the scathing words of his old friend. For a moment Dan thought some of the tension seemed to go out of his body and he swept past Al without a word and went out into the darkness. A moment later the soft clop of his horse could be heard as he rode out of town.

Dan looked hard at Rockhill. 'Clint has seen to things over at the hotel, you can take the matter up with the undertaker.' Rockhill nodded, turned and made for the door. 'Just a minute,' called Dan halting the rancher as his hand closed round the knob. 'I'd fergit those threats if I was you,' the sheriff added, his tone leaving no misunderstanding as to what would happen if Rockhill stepped out of line.

Without a word Rockhill flung open the door and left the office.

Dan looked at Jack and Howard. 'He might do anythin' the mood he's in,' he said grimly. 'Better follow him until you're satisfied he's headin' home.'

The brothers hurried from the office and rode after Rockhill whom they could hear galloping out of Red Springs.

Pete Hawksley rode slowly along the trail.

He was worried about his son and saddened by the attitude of his friend. The whole business had been a terrible shock to Hawksley and he was so preoccupied with his thoughts that he did not notice the pound of hoofs until the rider was close to him. He turned in the saddle to see who was behind him but he realized too late that it was Al Rockhill. Hawksley threw up his arms in defence but already Rockhill was alongside him and throwing himself from the saddle. His powerful frame crashed into Hawksley who was sent flying from his horse to hit the hard ground with Rockhill on top of him.

As they rolled over Hawksley pushed with his knees sending Rockhill rolling further. Hawksley struggled to push himself to his feet but Rockhill, in spite of his bulk, shoved himself upwards and in a flash leaped forward at Hawksley who had scarcely gained his feet. Rockhill's huge fist crashed into Hawksley's face opening a cut across his cheek and sending him staggering backwards. Rockhill, a flaming wildness in his eyes, lunged after him. He drove his feet again at Hawksley but he half warded off the blow which glanced across his temple. Nevertheless the swiftness and momentum of the attack was sufficient to make Hawksley lose his balance. He crashed to the ground and with a yell of triumph Rockhill leaped on top of him. He pinioned Hawksley to the earth with his heavy body and smashed his ham-like fist into Hawksley's face raining blow after blow on the helpless man. Rockhill had lost all reason in his wildness for revenge and would have beaten his old friend to death if Jack and Howard Collins had not arrived in time.

As they galloped up and saw what was happening the brothers swung out of the saddles before their horses had scarcely slowed down, dropped to the ground and ran at the struggling men. They seized Rockhill by his shoulders dragging him roughly away from Hawksley. Rockhill struggled in his frenzy and it was a hard job for the two men to hold him. Suddenly Jack brought his hand with a vicious slap across Rockhill's face jerking his head backwards. The blow shook Rockhill and seemed to knock some of the wildness out of him. His struggling gradually stopped and, seizing the opportunity, Howard drew his Colt and pressed it hard into Rockhill's ribs.

'Calm down!' hissed Howard. 'Or this thing might go off.'

Jack turned to Hawksley who was in a

sitting position on the ground dabbing his face with his handkerchief. He helped the rancher to his feet and was horrified by the sight of Hawksley's battered face. One eye was badly puffed and an ugly cut oozed blood above the other. The cut on his cheek had opened wider and blood trickled from his battered swollen lips. A man with less strength than Hawksley would have been unconscious. He swayed on his feet momentarily and Jack supported him. Then he seemed to pull strength in to himself; he looked round, picked up his Stetson and slapped it across his legs beating the dust from it.

'Will you be all right to get home?' asked Jack.

'Sure, sure,' replied Hawksley. He pulled himself to his feet and glared contemptuously at Rockhill who would have leaped at him again but for the cold steel pressed into his ribs. Hawksley was about to speak but seemed to think better of it. Instead he turned away.

'If you're all right,' said Jack, 'get off home, we'll see Rockhill doesn't bother you again tonight.'

Hawksley nodded, climbed on to his horse and rode away.

The Collins brothers kept Rockhill where he was until the sound of Hawksley's horse had faded in the distance.

'Right,' snapped Howard, 'on your horse.' He prodded the man forward with his Colt. Rockhill shuffled forward and was reaching for his saddle when Jack stopped him.

'We won't go easy with you next time,' he rasped. 'Git home and git some sense into you.'

Rockhill glared at Jack but said nothing. He swung into the saddle, kicked his horse forward and rode off into the darkness.

Chapter Four

When Dan McCoy hurried into his office early the following morning Clint Schofield was already up. With a prisoner held on a murder charge the deputy had slept in the office and Dan was pleased that there had been no further disturbances.

'With the circuit judge not due for a fortnight we could be in for trouble,' he said to Clint. 'Rockhill's a hard-headed man an' I figure with his temper up there's nothin' he wouldn't do to see Mick swingin' at the end of a rope.'

'Surely he's got more sense than to take the law into his own hands,' said Clint.

'You never know,' replied Dan, 'so I'm goin' to take precautions an' ride to the Bar X an' see if Bill Collins will let me hev Jack an' Howard for a few days. It's a pity I didn't ask them to stay last night.'

Five minutes later Dan was setting his horse into a gallop on the south road out of Red Springs heading for his father-in-law's ranch not far from Wayman's Ford on the

Brazo River.

At the same moment five miles north of the town a posse of ten men headed by Al Rockhill were riding at a steady pace towards Red Springs. The rancher kept to this pace until they were half a mile from the town when he drew rein. His men pulled to a halt around him.

'We'll split up here,' he said. 'Drift into town casual like an' take up your positions along the sidewalks so that you're covering the jail. Ward, you know your position, at the back. Blackie Mason an' I will ride straight up to the jail; if we have any trouble you know what to do.'

The men nodded and set off for Red Springs whilst Al Rockhill and his foreman, Blackie Mason, waited for ten minutes before following. When Rockhill rode slowly down the dusty main street of the town he noted with satisfaction that his men had positioned themselves well and had the jail covered from all angles. With Blackie Mason beside him he pulled up his horse to a halt in front of the jail.

Inside the sheriff's office Clint Schofield sitting behind the desk glanced casually out of the window and saw two men turning their horses towards the rail. He was galvanized into action, sprang from his chair, grabbed a rifle, flung open the door and stepped outside. Rockhill and Mason were out of the saddles and turning towards the steps on to the sidewalk.

'Hold it,' snapped Clint, his rifle held menacingly at the two men. 'Stay right where you are.'

The men froze in their tracks. Rockhill with one foot on the bottom step leaned forward and smiled up at the deputy.

'Mornin', Schofield,' he said. 'I hope...'

'I want no trouble,' cut in Clint curtly, 'so I figure the best thing will be if you both git on your horses an' ride out of town.'

Rockhill straightened. 'Now we are both of the same mind,' he said with mock pleasantry. 'I don't want trouble either so I would advise you to hand over Mick Hawksley quietly.' He made as if to walk up the steps but Clint motioned with his rifle and halted him again. Rockhill's eyes narrowed, a serious look crossed his face. 'Don't git in my way, Schofield,' he hissed. 'That murderer in there is goin' to pay fer what he did.'

'Back off, Rockhill,' snapped Clint. 'Leave that decision to the circuit judge.'

'Circuit judge,' sneered Rockhill, 'more than likely strings will be pulled and

Hawksley will git off with a jail sentence. I say a life for a life an' I want that life now but only after he's been made to suffer in front of his father!'

Clint gasped, realizing the intention of the man. 'You'll hev to take him over my dead body,' snarled Clint.

'Maybe we'll do jest that,' said Rockhill. 'It looks as though you're on your own an' the jail's covered by men so you may as well let us take Hawksley without any trouble.'

Clint shot a glance along the street and noted Twisted M cowboys at various points. The deputy sheriff shrugged his shoulders as if resigned to the fact that he was beaten.

'C'm on then,' he said and turned to the door. Rockhill grinned and followed him. Suddenly Clint paused and swung round sharply. The rancher was taken unawares and bumped into the cold muzzle of the rifle. 'All right,' snarled Clint. 'Call your men off or I'll blast your inside out!'

Rockhill paled. He knew Clint Schofield would not hesitate to carry out his threat in the course of justice. Blackie Mason started to move his hand slowly towards his holster.

'Leave it!' snapped Clint detecting the movement.

Blackie let his hand drop by his side.

'Look here, Schofield,' began Rockhill to keep Clint's attention. 'I want that...'

'Shut up,' snapped Clint. 'Jest call your men off an' then...'

The words were cut short as a Colt crashed down on his head. Rockhill grabbed the rifle, stepped to one side and Clint pitched on to the wooden sidewalk.

'Nice work, Ward,' congratulated Al. 'Good job we took that precaution.'

'Sorry, I was so long,' apologized Ward. 'Back door was locked and it took a bit of handlin' so as not to make a noise.'

The Twisted M foreman was by their side. 'Git hold of his feet, Ward,' he instructed. 'We'll leave Mister Lawman to cool off in one of his own cells.' The two men lifted the unconscious form and, preceded by Rockhill, entered the sheriff's office.

Al found the key to the cells on the desk and in a few moments Clint was locked behind bars. When Mick saw the men enter the jail fear gripped his heart. He knew only one fate awaited him at the hands of Al Rockhill. As the rancher inserted the key and swung the cell door open Mick saw hate and a mad lust for revenge in Rockhill's eyes. Automatically Mick shrank against the wall of the cell as if this would prevent him being taken. The burly figure of the rancher seemed to fill the cell as he stepped forward. He towered over young Hawksley, an evil grin on his face. It was as if he did not recognize Mick as someone he had once thought a lot about. Suddenly he slashed the back of his broad, hairy hand across Mick's face. His head jerked sideways, a big red weal flaring across his cheek. He staggered alongside the wall. Rockhill grabbed him by the shirt and jerked him forward propelling him across the cell. As he crashed against the bars Rockhill was beside him pushing him roughly through the doorway.

'Git outside, you little runt,' snarled Rockhill. 'Your day of reckonin' has come.'

As Mick staggered out of the cell Blackie Mason gave him a shove which sent him flying into the sheriff's office. Regaining his balance he turned, half crouching prepared to try to fend off, at least momentarily, the fate which awaited him but he found a grinning Ward covering him with a Colt.

'That wouldn't be wise,' he hissed. 'An' I would hate to deprive Mister Rockhill of his pleasure at the Broken K.'

Mick straightened. His brain pounded as he realized Rockhill's intention. He turned to the rancher. 'I didn't kill Kathy,' he said, 'but if you're determined to hang an inno-cent man don't do it in front of my mother and father; spare them that.'

'Don't play the innocent with me,' snapped Rockhill. 'They're to blame as much as you.' He stepped forward, grabbed Mick by the shoulders and pushed him towards the door. As he reached the doorway he grabbed the woodwork for support but Blackie planted a boot in the small of Mick's back to send him flying across the sidewalk. He tumbled down the steps and sprawled face forwards in the dust. Slowly he pushed himself to his feet as the three men stood over him.

As soon as their boss appeared the Twisted M cowboys stepped from the sidewalks to their horses but still kept their guns menacing the few townsfolk who had been on the street and witnessed what had hap-pened. One cowboy hurried forward leading a horse to the small group of men outside the jail.

'Git mounted!' yelled Rockhill at Mick.

Hawksley shuffled forward and reluctantly mounted the animal. The cowboy passed the reins to him then ran back to his own horse and was ready to ride as Rockhill and his foreman closed on either side of Mick Hawksley and set the animals into a gallop along the main street. The Twisted M cowboys closed behind their boss and the posse thundered out of Red Springs along the north road.

As soon as the horsemen had left the street men raced to the jail hoping they would find Clint Schofield still alive. They burst into the building and soon carried the deputy sheriff into the office. Someone appeared with a bucket of cold water and a cloth. They applied the cold damp cloth to his head and before long Clint was revived. As his brain cleared and he regained his senses Clint sat up.

'How long have I been out?' he asked looking round desperately.

'Nearly ten minutes,' came the reply.

'Hell,' he cried scrambling to his feet. 'I hope I won't be too late.' His head swam and he grasped the nearest person for support. In spite of protestations he pushed his way to the door insisting that he must ride for Dan. He untied his horse from the rail, pulled himself into the saddle and turned the animal to head along the south road out of town.

Although his head was throbbing he kept the horse to a fast gallop, desperately searching the landscape ahead for sight of Dan. He had ridden about three miles before he saw three riders in the distance. He urged the horse faster and was relieved when he noticed the three men quicken their pace for he knew they must have recognized him. Just before reaching them Clint pulled his horse to a dust-raising, sliding halt and then turned the animal alongside Dan and the Collins brothers urging them to keep riding fast.

'What's happened?' yelled Dan, concern in his voice.

'Rockhill busted Mick out of jail,' shouted Clint. 'I had the drop on him but someone got me from behind. I figure they're headin' fer the Broken K.'

At the mention of the Broken K Dan automatically changed the direction of the ride and headed across the grassland so that they would cut across the west side of Red Springs and save going through the town.

'Head fer town, an' git that wound attended to,' called Dan indicating the con-gealed blood on the back of Clint's head.

The deputy shook his head. 'Comin' with you,' he yelled above the pound of the hoofs. 'I don't like being made a fool of.'

Earth flew under the thundering hoofs as the four men settled down into a fast ride for the Broken K ranch.

Al Rockhill kept to a steady but fast pace northwards. Riders remained close to Mick Hawksley so that there was no chance of him making a break for it. Four miles along the trail they topped a rise and Rockhill suddenly pulled his mount to a halt. The other riders were not slow to follow suit and brought their horses milling around their boss. Some distance across the grassland a lone rider had pulled his horse to a stop at the sight of the posse. Rockhill pulled a spy glass from its leather and trained it on the rider. Suddenly the horseman turned his mount and kicked it into a gallop.

'Broken K hand,' called Rockhill. 'Reckon he's recognized us. Ward, Clay, git him, but no killin'.'

The two men kicked their horses forward setting them across the grassland at a tangent to the rider's trail. Hoofs flew across the ground and when the Broken K cowboy saw he was being pursued he lashed his horse for greater effort but the animal had had a tiring morning and, in spite of its efforts, the Twisted M men gained on him. Slowly the angle closed and when Ward and Clay reached his track they were just a few yards behind him. Now the strength of the powerful Twisted M horses made itself felt and the gap closed quickly.

In desperation the man reached for his Colt but it was too late. His pursuers were alongside him and Ward flung himself from his horse's back. His shoulder crashed into the Broken K rider's side and his arms encircled his waist dragging him from the saddle. Both men crashed to the ground in a heap their breath driven from their bodies. Ward had braced himself for the fall and twisted free of the entanglement quickly. He jumped to his feet and, seeing the man still holding his Colt, lashed out with his foot kicking it from his grasp. His own Colt leaped to his hand.

'All right, on your feet,' he snapped.

Slowly and dejectedly the man pushed himself from the ground and stood looking grimly at Ward whilst they waited for Clay who had ridden after the two riderless horses. He brought them under control quickly and returned to the waiting men.

'Into the saddle,' ordered Ward motioning with his Colt.

Reluctantly the cowboy climbed on to his horse and the three men turned their horses to meet the rest of the Twisted M outfit.

'Nice work,' congratulated Rockhill as they rode up. 'Now the element of surprise is still ours.' He looked at Mick and the Broken K hand. 'Don't try anythin',' he added, 'or some finger might get too itchy.'

The two men said nothing and the posse set off on its grim task.

It was a grim, sore-faced Pete Hawksley that faced his wife, Betty, in the kitchen of their ranch-house.

'I wish I'd kept the hands back,' he said. 'I'd hev busted Mick out of jail an' got out of here.'

Betty, pale-faced, in her early fifties, spun round on her husband. 'Then I'm glad you've had to send them for that herd,' she said. 'And don't get any fool notion of trying it yourself. It's bad enough having Mick in trouble, I don't want you in jail as well.'

'But...' started Pete.

'No buts,' cut in Betty. 'You say Mick didn't do it; if you believe that you'll let the law take care of things. He'll get a fair trial.'

'Maybe,' replied Pete. 'But things are stacked against him.'

'He didn't do it so there must be a loophole somewhere,' said Betty. 'Get the best lawyer you can, I feel sure he'd...'

Her words were cut short by the sound of approaching horses. She glanced out of the window and was horrified by what she saw. Her eyes widened with fear; she swayed and leaned against the wall.

'Oh, no, no, not that,' she moaned.

Pete, wondering what was the matter, was by her side in a flash, supporting her with his arm around her shoulder. He stiffened when he saw his son surrounded by a posse of Twisted M cowboys led by Al Rockhill approaching the ranch.

'You'd better stay inside, Betty,' he said grimly and turned to hurry out of the house but his wife followed him, feeling she could not stand inside and watch.

As they stepped out on to the verandah Jim Masters, the Broken K foreman, and Burt Weldon who had been breaking some horse in a nearby corral came running up with Colts drawn.

'They've got Mick,' called Masters. 'Do we fight?'

Pete shook his head sadly. 'It would be useless; there are not enough of us, beside they hold a trump card in Mick, an' I see they must hev picked up Jed on the range.'

Jim Masters and Burt Weldon saw the sense in Hawksley's words, holstered their guns and watched the posse as it approached slowly.

Al Rockhill deliberately slowed the pace as they neared the ranch so that Mick's parents would suffer longer with their thoughts for he knew they would have guessed the intention of the band of men that was riding towards them. He halted his men in front of the verandah.

Suddenly Betty Hawksley dashed forward and grabbed Al's stirrup. 'Let my boy go,' she sobbed, her voice almost choking in her throat. 'Let him go.' Tears streamed down her face. 'What are you going to do with him?'

Al Rockhill looked down coldly on the lady he had once counted as a very dear friend. 'I've no quarrel with you, Betty, please go inside and don't see what's goin' to happen. I blame Pete for not takin' his boy in hand sooner.'

'Don't do it, Al, don't do it,' she pleaded. She lifted her tear-stained face towards her son, who, in spite of the threat which hung over him, mustered a smile for his mother. She looked back at Rockhill. 'You've no wife of your own,' she said, 'So you've no idea how this is making me suffer. Please, Al, let the law deal with him. If you kill him here you'll kill me from the inside.'

'How do you think I felt when I heard

about Kathy?' replied Rockhill. 'My world collapsed; you'll still hev Pete but I hev no one.' He turned to one of his men and before Betty could speak again he ordered him to take her inside the house.

The man swung from the saddle and took Mrs Hawksley firmly by the arm and led her sobbing to the house.

Pete stepped forward, hate in his eyes as he moved towards his old friend. 'If you do this, Al, I'll hound you fer the rest of your life,' he hissed. 'Remember what I did fer you when you came to these parts?' he added hoping to sway Rockhill from the course he seemed determined to take.

'I'll always be grateful for that,' replied Rockhill, 'but it's all been a waste of time, your boy took away the one person for whom I'd spent my whole time building up the ranch.' His voice rose in anger. 'Hanging's too good for him; he ought to be flogged first an' that is just what is goin' to happen an' you're goin' to stand there an' watch it all.'

Pete recoiled at the horror behind Al's words. His hand automatically flew for his Colt but Blackie Mason already had his gun out. The roar of the Colt and the crash of the bullet close to his feet made Pete

Hawksley's hand freeze on the butt of his Colt. Al Rockhill nodded and two of his men climbed from their horses, relieved Pete of his gun and held his arms in a vice-like grip. Another man took the Colts from Jim Masters and Burt Weldon and kept them covered with his own gun.

Al Rockhill swung from his horse and this was a signal to two more of his cowboys to leave their saddles. They crossed to Mick Hawksley and dragged him from his horse, tumbling him into a heap in the dust. They pulled him unceremoniously to his feet and dragged him roughly to the rails of the verandah. They tied his hands over the top rail and looping a short rope round Mick's neck pulled his head downwards tying the rope round the bottom rail so that Mick's back was bent to receive the lash.

Pete Hawksley struggled in vain to release himself from the strong grips which held him to go to his son's aid.

Rockhill turned to his foreman who handed him a whip. Both men swung to the ground and walked towards Mick Hawksley. Blackie Mason grasped Mick's shirt by the neck and with a powerful jerk ripped it open the full length of his back then tore it roughly from Mick's body. As Rockhill turned to take up his position Pete Hawksley found himself some super strength and tore himself free from the two cowboys who held him. He leaped forward flinging himself at Rockhill and crashed his fist into Rockhill's face to send him staggering sideways. Before Pete Hawksley could follow up his attack the two cowboys jumped forward dragging him into the dust. He struggled, but was pulled roughly to his feet to face Rockhill who stood staring at him angrily as he wiped the trickle of blood from the corner of his mouth.

'If you use that whip on my boy my outfit will hit you so hard that you'll face ruin!' screamed Hawksley. 'We'll tear your place apart an' I'll not rest until you lick the dirt off my boots!'

Rockhill ignored the threats and signalled to his men to get Hawksley out of the way. They dragged him forcibly backwards until he was in such a position close to his son that he would see every whip mark as it was made on Mick's back.

The owner of the Twisted M estimated the distance carefully, positioning himself for the maximum effect. He gripped the handle of the whip firmly; the long rawhide thong lay snake-like in the dust in front of him. Pete

Hawksley's protestations ceased as he realized how determined Rockhill was and that there was nothing more he could do to stop this terrible thing happening. A frightening silence settled over the grim scene.

Rockhill flicked his powerful wrist and the whip lash jerked into the dust behind him. He balanced himself carefully, tensing himself to deliver the first blow.

Suddenly the silence was shattered by the crash of a rifle. The dust spurted as the bullet hit the ground close to Rockhill's feet. He jumped as if he had been stung. Everyone spun round to see four horsemen, their rifles covering the group, lined up a short distance away. Hands flew towards their Colts but froze before they touched the butts as a rifle crashed again sending a bullet whining over their heads.

Dan McCoy, Clint Schofield and the Collins brothers put their horses into a slow walk towards the ranch-house. Dan muttered instructions and his three companions halted close to the group ranging themselves so that every man was covered by their rifles. The sheriff kept his horse moving towards Rockhill. His eyes never left the rancher, and he kept his rifle pointing straight at him.

'Drop that whip,' ordered Dan curtly as he

stopped his horse beside Rockhill.

The rancher, his face black with anger and annoyance at being prevented from taking his revenge, released his grip on the whip which fell into the dust at his feet.

Dan swung from the saddle and eyed Rockhill coldly. 'Cut Mick loose,' he snapped.

Rockhill shuffled forward to the verandah, drew a knife from his belt and with two sharp slashes freed his prisoner. As Mick straightened, the door of the house burst open and Betty Hawksley, tears still in her eyes, but a look of relief on her face, rushed out and flung her arms round her son. She looked over his shoulder at the sheriff.

'Thank goodness you got here in time,' she gasped gratefully.

'If we hadn't there would have been other people on a murder charge,' said Dan looking hard at Rockhill. 'I could still clap you in jail for busting Mick out,' he added, 'but as far as I can see that would serve no useful purpose; you know you were on the wrong side of the law…'

'Isn't he a murderer?' shouted Rockhill pointing in the direction of young Hawksley. 'I want justice, and I want it quick.'

'Rockhill,' snapped Dan angrily, 'I've

stood enough nonsense over this. I want no more trouble from either you or Hawksley. You'll both hev justice but at the proper time, when the circuit judge comes in a fortnight. If there's any more trouble I'll clamp whoever causes it in jail, until the judge comes.' He looked hard at Rockhill. 'Now git yourself and your men out of here.'

Al Rockhill turned to his horse and mounted. He glared at Dan then pulled the animal round and led his men away from the Broken K.

Dan watched them out of sight before he turned to Mick. 'Guess I'd better git you back to jail,' he said.

Mick nodded and kissed his mother. 'Don't worry,' he said. 'Everything will be all right, but I wish I could remember what happened.'

As the sheriff's party rode away Pete Hawksley turned to the man whom Rockhill had captured on the range.

'Jed,' he said, 'with Rockhill in the mood he's in he might do anythin' fer revenge. Ride north to warn our outfit to look out fer that herd.'

Chapter Five

The following day Kathy was buried in the tiny cemetery on the edge of Red Springs and Al Rockhill returned to the Twisted M, bitterness eating out his heart. He had just entered the house and poured himself a large whisky when there was a knock on the door and his foreman Blackie Mason entered the room.

'I just want you to know, Mister Rockhill that all the men are behind you,' he said. 'In spite of what the sheriff said yesterday we'll be ridin' right with you if you want to go after the Hawksleys again.'

'Thanks,' replied Rockhill handing his foreman a glass of whisky, 'but I realize that I was wrong yesterday; I could have put a noose around some of your necks. We'll wait; if justice isn't done then we'll ride again. There's plenty to keep me occupied on the ranch until the trial; I'll ride with you to the branding tomorrow.'

The following day Al was up early and shortly after eight o'clock headed for the

75

range with his cowboys leaving only two of them at the ranch repairing fences.

It was mid-morning and the two men were hard at work when they were startled by the pound of hoofs. They looked up and were shaken to see six masked men riding hard towards them. Instinctively they reached for their Colts but as they did so a rifle crashed and bullets whined close to them. They spun to see another man standing beside his horse a short distance behind them. They eased their hands away from their Colts as the leading horseman pulled to a halt in front of them.

'Wise men,' he said. 'We don't want any killing.'

He waved to the seventh man who led his horse up behind them. He jerked their Colts from their holsters then brought the butt of his rifle hard against each man's head. They tumbled into the dust without a sound.

'Right,' shouted the leader. 'Git to it.'

The masked men swung to the ground and whilst some started to tear down the fences others hurried to the ranch-house and bunk-house determined to wreck the buildings.

Things had been going well out on the

range but Al Rockhill decided that it would be wiser if they had some more horses so as not to work any one horse too hard in the task of cutting out the cattle that needed branding. He called out Ward and Clay and the three men set off for the ranch.

As they topped the rise a short distance from the ranch-house Al Rockhill gasped with surprise and drew hard on the reins.

'What the hell's goin' on?' cried the rancher as the other two riders pulled up alongside him. 'C'm on!' he yelled suddenly, kicking his horse into a fast gallop down the slope. Earth flew under the flashing hoofs as the three horsemen thundered towards the ranch.

The four men who were tearing down the fences looked up in alarm when they heard the pound of hoofs. One of them raced for the house, yelling at the top of his voice to warn his companions. The other three men ran to their horses, grabbed their rifles and started to fire in the direction of the three riders even though they were still out of effective range. As the masked men ran from the house their leader sized up the situation in a flash.

'Hold them off,' he yelled to the three men with the rifles. 'We must git Rockhill's horses!'

He led his men to their mounts and once in the saddles they were soon at the corral which held ten horses. The leader leaned from the saddle and swiftly unfastened the gate. Two of his men rode into the corral and as they drove the horses out the animals were taken under control quickly and driven at a fast pace away from the Twisted M.

When the bullets began to whine around Rockhill and his two men they hauled hard on the reins bringing their mounts to a sliding halt. They turned into a slight depression, dropped from the saddles, flattened themselves on the ground and returned the rifle fire. Suddenly Rockhill stiffened.

'They're takin' the horses' he yelled. 'We'll hev to try to work our way round to the left.'

Their three horses had moved some distance away and when the three men tried to work their way out of the depression towards them they were immediately sent scurrying back by a withering hail of fire from the three masked men. They then kept up a steady stream of bullets keeping Rockhill and his two men pinned down in the depression whilst the rest of the gang made off with the horses.

Suddenly the firing ceased. Rockhill waited

a moment then carefully peered over the top of the depression. The rancher leaped to his feet.

'C'm on,' he yelled, 'they're pulling out.'

He was already racing for his horse as Wade and Clay jumped to their feet. In a matter of a few minutes they had regained their horses but the masked men had already got a good start on them and as for the men with his horses Rockhill knew that he had no chance of catching up with them. His only hope was to catch one of the three men now galloping away from the Twisted M and make him talk.

He called to his horse for greater effort and the powerful animal stretched itself, pounding the earth in fast pursuit. As he thundered past the ranch with Wade and Clay close on his heels Rockhill saw that they had gained a little on the men in front.

'We'll git them,' he yelled triumphantly and kept urging his horse onwards.

They maintained the earth-tearing pace for three miles when they lost sight of their quarry as the three men disappeared over a slight rise in the undulating grassland. Rockhill's powerful animal took the incline in its stride and was in full gallop when it topped the rise. The raiders had turned from their track and were heading across the grassland in a different direction. Rockhill, without thinking, pulled hard on the reins and at the same time turned his horse. Wade and Clay were close behind in full gallop and Rockhill's action took them completely by surprise. Wade tried in vain to avoid disaster, but the two animals crashed into each other, horseflesh rearing against horseflesh. With cries of terror the animals were sent hurtling to the ground by the suddenness and power of the impact. Rockhill and Wade were flung from the saddles and crashed heavily on the ground. Clay, who had overrun them in the onward rush, hauled hard on the reins bringing his horse to an earth-tearing, sliding halt. He turned his horse and was out of the saddle in a flash. He leaped to Rockhill's side and dropped on one knee to see that his boss, with an ugly gash across his head, was unconscious. Glancing up he saw that Wade in a daze was struggling to sit up. Clay raced to his horse, grabbed a canteen of water and ran to Wade. The cowboy, who was holding his head in his hands looked up weakly at Clay who forced some water between his lips, then, soaking his neckerchief, dowsed Wade's forehead.

'You all right?' asked Clay anxiously.

Wade nodded. 'Just dazed, don't feel to hev broken anythin'. How's the boss?'

'Out cold,' replied Clay, 'but I reckon he'll be all right.' He helped Wade to his feet and handed him the canteen of water. 'Hev a look at him whilst I see to these two horses.'

Wade nodded and walked slowly towards his boss. Clay crossed to Rockhill's horse which still lay on the ground and it required only a quick glance on Clay's part to see that the animal had broken its leg. Reluctantly Clay drew his Colt; he loved horses and, although he knew that nothing could be done for the animal, he hesitated before he squeezed the trigger. Sickened he turned away and hurried to Wade's horse which was standing a few yards away frightened by the accident. The roar of the Colt had caused it to trot further away but Clay soothed it by calling to it as he approached. The cowboy was relieved to find that the horse was all right except for a few cuts. He spent a few minutes soothing the animal before hurrying to Wade who was busy bathing Rockhill's wound. Clay examined the rancher quickly and was satisfied that no bones were broken. Five minutes passed before Rockhill's eyes flickered open during which time Clay had bound the wound with a neckerchief. Rockhill struggled to sit up but Clay pressed him to lie still for a few minutes. Slowly his mind cleared and when the cowboy saw that his boss had regained his senses he helped him to his feet. Wade hurried to get the two remaining horses and when he returned Rockhill apologized for what had happened.

'I guess those raidin' coyotes hev got clean away,' he concluded cursing himself for his own carelessness.

Clay helped him on to his horse then climbed up behind him to lend support for the ride back to the Twisted M.

Dan McCoy kept his horse to a steady lope as he turned it down the hillside towards the Twisted M ranch. His eyes narrowed and a puzzled frown crossed his brow when he saw the broken fences. He was also surprised that there was no sign of life but on nearing the house he noticed two cowboys sitting on the steps holding their heads. They glanced up when they heard the clop of horse's hoofs but showed little enthusiasm when they saw the sheriff.

'What's happened here?' asked Dan as he swung from the saddle in front of the house.

'We were jumped by a masked gang,'

muttered one of the men.

'What!' Dan gasped.

'They've sure played havoc around here,' went on the cowboy.

'So I see,' said Dan. 'An' they weren't easy on your heads,' he added when he saw the deep gashes, caused by the rifle.

'They've been inside the house as well,' put in the other cowboy.

Dan entered the house and was astonished at the destruction which had been caused.

'Did you recognize any of them?' asked Dan when he returned to the verandah. The men shook their heads. 'Seems as if they might have been interrupted,' said Dan. 'One of the rooms hasn't been touched.'

'I don't know about that,' muttered one of the men, 'they had time to rustle some horses.'

'We haven't had any rustling around here fer a long time,' pointed out Dan, 'must be a gang that's just moved into the area.' He paused thoughtfully. He could not understand why rustlers should want to smash the place down. 'Where's Rockhill?' he asked suddenly.

'On the range, at the brandin',' came the reply.

'Will you be all right whilst I take a look

round?' asked Dan. 'Then, I'll ride an' get Rockhill.'

The men nodded and for ten minutes Dan searched round the ranch-house without finding anything of great help. When he returned to the two men he held out his hand on which rested some spent cartridge cases.

'I found these just over there,' he replied. 'Any Twisted M men been using a rifle this morning.'

'No,' came the answer. 'Everyone was away early, we were left to repair fences an' we certainly didn't use a rifle.'

'Then I figure someone interrupted these raiders an' they had to put up a fight,' mused Dan, 'an' yet it looks as if they got clean away. Guess I'll take a look round a bit further afield.'

He was about to move away when he stopped. Shading his eyes against the sun he saw what at first he thought were two riders approaching the ranch slowly. Suddenly he gasped when he realized one of the horses carried two men. Dan swung to meet the approaching riders.

'What happened to you?' he called as he turned alongside Clay and Rockhill.

Rockhill, who was feeling much better,

quickly told the sheriff what had happened.

'If you don't need my help I reckon I'll see if I can pick up their trail,' he said at the conclusion of Rockhill's story.

'You git after them,' replied Rockhill. 'I want my horses back.'

Dan nodded but before he turned his horse he shot one last question at the powerfully built rancher. 'Know anyone who'd want to wreck your house?'

'Wreck my house?' said Rockhill surprise showing on his face. Suddenly he realized what must have happened. 'Hawksley!' he snapped.

Dan said nothing but turned his horse sharply and kicked it into a gallop. His thoughts troubled him as he rode across the grassland. Rustling and destruction did not mix; he had heard Hawksley threaten Rockhill and Hawksley could be behind the smashing of the buildings but Hawksley would not rustle horses; if they were found on his land it would condemn him straight away. Dan's mind turned over the facts wondering if there could be any connection between this raid and the murder of Kathy Rockhill.

When he reached the point where Rockhill had met with his accident he searched the ground carefully and after about half an hour picked up what he reckoned was more than likely the trail of the rustlers. He followed it for some time but progress was slow and eventually, when he lost it altogether, he decided that he had better return to Red Springs. The trail appeared to be leading to the hills to the north but he had not the time to ride there now on the off-chance of finding the rustlers. Reluctantly he turned his horse and headed for Red Springs.

After two miles he decided to call on Pete Hawksley on his way back and was soon pulling up outside the Broken K ranchhouse. Pete Hawksley hurried out to meet him.

'Hope you're bringing good news,' he called lightly.

Dan shook his head. 'Sorry,' he replied. His face was so serious that the smile vanished from Hawksley's face and a puzzled look took its place. The sheriff went on to tell him what had happened at the Twisted M.

'Know anythin' about it?' asked Dan as he finished his story.

Hawksley was taken aback at the sheriff's suspicions. 'Of course not,' he snapped. 'Besides, it's impossible, there are only three of us here, Jim Masters, Burt Weldon and myself; the rest of the boys are collecting a herd up north.'

Before Dan could reply the sound of a galloping horse could be heard and both men turned to see Al Rockhill, his head still bandaged, riding towards them.

Rockhill pulled up in front of the house and glared at Hawksley. 'I realized I was wrong to take the law into my own hands when I came here the other day; I was prepared to wait and let the law take its own course. But now after what you've done to my place I'm prepared to fight you if that's what you want.'

'Hold it, Rockhill,' snapped Dan. 'Hawksley couldn't have done it; there are only three men here, the rest are away bringing a herd from the north.'

Rockhill laughed scornfully. 'Hawksley's crafty enough to hev hired a gang an' put them in the hills,' he said. 'He'll hear more from me!' Rockhill pulled his horse round sharply and, before anyone could reply, kicked it into a gallop away from the Broken K.

Chapter Six

Pete Hawksley had much to think about that night and when he announced to his wife the next morning that he was going to ride to Fort Worth to engage an eminent lawyer to defend Mick she was pleased.

'I'm a little apprehensive after Al's threat yesterday,' he concluded, 'but I'm sure he would not harm you, Betty. I'll hev a word with Masters and Weldon before I leave; they'll see you're all right.'

After breakfast Pete strolled to the corral where Jim Masters and Burt Weldon were busy breaking some new horses. He leaned on the rail watching them for a few minutes counting his good luck at having two such good horse wranglers. Masters had been with Hawksley for five years, he was good looking in a rugged way, a pleasant man who was respected by the rest of Hawksley's outfit. Weldon, who had been with the Broken K less than a year, was about twenty-three but looked older than his years. He was five feet ten in height but equally as strong as his tall powerful foreman. Although Hawksley had not taken to the man when he had ridden in looking for a job, and even now knew him no better than that first day, he had so admired the way he handled horses that he had hired him.

The two men were about to rope another horse when Hawksley called them over.

'I'll be away a couple of days,' explained Pete. 'I'm goin' to Fort Worth to hire a lawyer. Rockhill threatened me again yesterday so keep your eyes open. Don't fight him; just see my wife is not harmed if he should show up.'

'We'll look after things,' replied Masters but Weldon's face was impassive beneath his shaggy eyebrows as he mopped his forehead with his neckerchief.

When Pete Hawksley arrived in Red Springs he stopped outside the sheriff's office, swung from the saddle and strode into the building to find Dan McCoy, Clint Schofield and the Collins brothers discussing the recent raid on the Twisted M. After exchanging the usual greeting Hawksley explained the reason for his call.

'I was just passing through,' he said, 'on my way to Fort Worth to engage a lawyer to defend Mick.'

'A very sensible idea,' agreed Dan. 'Call on Lance Peters – he's the best you'll find.'

'Thanks, Dan,' said Pete. 'I hope this nasty mess is soon cleared up.'

Dan nodded. 'Like to see Mick before you go?' he asked.

'Sure would,' replied Pete, and Clint took him through to the cells.

Dan had a thoughtful five minutes waiting for Pete to return and when the rancher came back into the office and was about to go with a word of thanks Dan stopped him.

'I'd like to see Lance Peters before he reaches Red Springs,' said Dan. 'Tell him to leave Fort Worth on the stage next Tuesday; that'll give him a week here before the trial's due; I'll ride out an' meet it at Mineral Wells an' ride back to town with Lance.'

Peter Hawksley agreed and left Red Springs in a happier frame of mind. His thoughts would have been disturbed as he neared Fort Worth had he known that a shadowy figure rode from the Broken K in the gathering darkness. The rider halted in a little hollow half way to the Twisted M and waited to keep a rendezvous which had been kept every night for a month before Kathy's murder. Five minutes passed before another rider emerged from the darkness. Greetings were exchanged, instructions issued then both riders disappeared into the darkness, one of them heading for the hills north of the Twisted M spread.

It was early the following day that a band of seven men pulled their horses to a halt on the edge of some low hills overlooking a wide shallow valley.

'We're just in time,' grinned their leader when he saw a straggling herd of cattle making its way slowly along the valley. 'We'll hit them hard an' fast; cut off about hundred and fifty head and drive them fast back through these hills.'

'Suppose we're followed,' said one of the gang.

'Try and stampede the rest of the herd,' replied the leader, 'but I want Butch, Ted an' Wes to hang back an' take any action necessary if we are followed but I hope the stampede will keep the Broken K hombres busy.'

The men pulled their neckerchiefs up over the lower half of their faces. The leader watched the herd carefully and when he was satisfied that it was in the best position for attack he gave the signal to move off. Kicking their horses forward the men moved down the slope using a fold in the hillside to hide their presence from the unsuspecting Broken K cowboys. By the time they reached the bottom of the hillside they were fairly close to the herd and they burst from the slope at a fast gallop taking the cowboys completely by surprise. Almost before they realized what was happening the cowboys riding alongside the herd were over-run by the masked men yelling at the top of their voices and firing their Colts. Startled by the sudden change in the peaceful trek the cattle seemed to heave as one mass and broke into a run. Steer pushed against steer sending its neighbour forward into a run to try to escape the sudden thrust on the side of the herd. The masked men turned alongside the cattle forcing the centre of the herd to move way from their pressure and leaving a bulge of cattle in front and to the right. Skilfully the leader and three of his men cut this block of cattle off from the main herd which the rest of the gang forced onwards into a dead run. Bellowing cattle tore onwards at ever in-creasing speed and, satisfied that the herd could not be held, the masked men turned their attention to the steers which had been cut away from the main herd.

Things had happened so quickly that apart from two or three Broken K cowboys no one else knew for a moment what had happened. As the steers started to run Stan Mills, who was in charge of the drive, saw the masked men. He shouted orders quickly, realizing that the herd was breaking into a stampede. Mills led three men at an earth-pounding gallop towards the raiders but already they had split the herd and were driving about a hundred and fifty steers towards the hills. Bullets flew around the Broken K men and when he saw one of them hit in the shoulder Mills eased the pace. He glanced back at the herd now in full run and he realised that the rest of the outfit would need all the help they could get. It was hard to see cattle being stolen without making some effort to stop them but Mills realized that, compared to the number which had been taken, the rest of the herd was more important. He drew rein hard shouting to the rest of his men to get back to the herd. Mills hesitated; he knew his ramrod could handle things, and, not liking being outsmarted, he turned his horse to follow the raiders. Knowing it was useless to close with the rustlers on his own Mills was content to follow at a leisurely pace hoping that by finding the gang's hide-out he would be able to retake the cattle later.

The raiders kept to a good pace as they moved through the hills and Mills was a little puzzled by the fact that they made no attempt to conceal their progress. He was left in no doubt as to why, when, after riding a further mile, three masked riders with Colts drawn appeared from behind a huge outcrop of rock and barred his path. He was tempted to kick his horse into a gallop to try to break through them but he realized it would be useless and he cursed himself for not thinking that some of the raiders would hang back in case they were followed. He looked hard at the men hoping that he might see something which would identify them but he saw nothing. One of the men moved forward towards him, drew alongside and relieved Mills of his Colt and his rifle. As he did so Mills stiffened when he saw the Twisted M brand on the horse!

Before the Broken K man knew what was happening the masked man brought the muzzle of his Colt crashing across the side of his head to pitch him from the saddle unconscious into the dust. The three masked men pulled their horses round and sent them galloping after the rest of the gang.

The sun was nearing the horizon when Jim

Masters and Burt Weldon were attracted by the thrum of horse's hoofs. They looked questioningly at each other then as one man drew their Colts and hurried to the ranch-house. After warning Mrs Hawksley that someone was approaching they positioned themselves close to the front door and waited as the beat of the hoofs grew louder.

'Stan Mills!' gasped Masters when the rider came in sight. 'Wonder what's happened at the herd.'

The two men replaced their Colts and stepped from the verandah to meet Mills who kept his horse at full gallop until close to the house. Masters saw at once that the horse had been ridden hard; the animal was about at the end of its strength. The Broken K foreman could almost sense the relief in the animal when its rider pulled it to a halt and swung quickly from the saddle. Alarm showed on Masters' face as he faced the dust-covered sweating Mills across whose head blood had congealed in an ugly gash.

Mill stumbled and Masters and Weldon jumped forward to support him. His knees felt weak and his head spun after the hard ride in the heat of the day. His chest heaved as he gulped in air to ease his aching lungs. The door of the house burst open and Mrs

Hawksley, concern and alarm showing in her face, hurried on to the verandah. One glance at the wounded man was enough.

'Bring him inside,' she instructed.

The two men helped Mills up the steps and into the house. Mills tried to speak but the effort seemed to be too much at the moment.

'Get him some brandy from the sideboard,' Mrs Hawksley told Masters and then hurried away to return a few moments later with a bowl of warm water.

As she bathed his head and face Weldon supported the wounded man and helped him with his glass. The brandy scorched his throat and seemed to drive new life into his weary body. Mrs Hawksley tended to the wound quickly and efficiently and soon had it neatly bound. It was only when Masters felt that Mills was fit to talk that the Broken K foreman allowed him to do so.

'Masked men raided the Twisted M, and Rockhill blamed us; now masked men on Twisted M horses, hit our herd,' mused Masters when Mills had finished his story. He paused thoughtfully then turned to Mrs Hawksley. 'When are you expecting Mister Hawksley back?' he asked.

'He thought some time tomorrow,' replied

Mrs Hawksley, 'but I don't expect he will arrive until late afternoon.'

'Then I think I'd better ride to Red Springs and let the sheriff know,' said the foreman. 'He won't be able to do anythin' today; it will soon be dark, but he may want to take action in the morning.'

Mrs Hawksley thought it would be a wise thing to do and before leaving the house Masters instructed Weldon to keep an eye on things at the ranch until he returned.

After Pete Hawksley had left Red Springs for Fort Worth Dan McCoy had spent the rest of the day trying to find some clue to the unknown person he felt sure had visited the hotel room used by Mick Hawksley, but without success. He had been equally un-successful the following day trying to get a lead on the masked men who had raided the Twisted M. Neither Clint Schofield nor the Collins brothers had been able to turn up any clue which might be useful.

With darkness covering the Texas country-side and the night life of Red Springs in full swing the four men were seated in the sheriff's office discussing the two crimes and trying to find something to connect them. Dan was puzzled and yet he had a feeling he had overlooked something which would link them both together.

The door opened and the four men looked up, surprised to see Jim Masters walk in.

'Howdy, Jim, what brings you here at this time of night?' greeted Dan. 'Thought you'd be needed at the ranch with your boss away.'

'The herd our boys are bringin' down from the north was hit by masked raiders an' about a hundred and fifty head run off,' replied Jim.

'What!' gasped Dan. 'The masked gang again.'

The other three men were equally surprised.

'And they were ridin' Twisted M horses!' added Masters.

The four men listened thoughtfully as the Broken K foreman related his story. 'We can do nothin' tonight,' said Dan when Masters had finished his story. 'Clint, I'd like you ride out to the hills to the north of the Twisted M, you know them well, an' see if you can pick up anything on this gang.'

'Why not tackle Rockhill?' suggested Jack Collins. 'They were his horses.'

'Horses were taken when his ranch was raided,' pointed out Howard.

'Rockhill accused Hawksley but I can't see him raiding his own herd, an' the same applies to Rockhill, I can't see him smashing up his own ranch, but they are both in such moods that they'll accuse each other an' say they raided themselves as a blind,' said Dan. 'But in any case I'll visit Rockhill tomorrow after Hawksley gits back from Fort Worth.'

It was late the following afternoon when Pete Hawksley rode into Red Springs to find Dan McCoy anxiously awaiting his return.

'Lance Peters has taken the case,' Hawksley announced, 'and he agreed it was a good idea for you to meet him on the stage on Tuesday.'

'Good,' replied Dan, 'but I'm afraid I've some bad news fer you.' He went on to tell Pete of the rustling.

'So this is Al's first blow,' he hissed, 'but I'll git even with him.'

'Now hold it, Pete,' said Dan. 'Remember Al accused you of stealin' some of his horses.'

'You don't think I raided myself,' replied Pete in astonishment. 'More like one of Al's tricks makin' out his horses were stolen.'

Dan did not bother to reply to that statement but informed Pete that he was riding out to the Twisted M and wanted him to go along with him.

Pete readily agreed and in a few minutes

the two men were heading out of Red Springs, by the north road.

They kept to a steady pace across the grassland and when they were passing a herd of cattle Hawksley suddenly hauled his horse to a halt. Dan halted his horse and turned it back alongside Pete who was staring at the herd.

'Some of those beeves look trail weary to me,' he said and sent his horse towards them. He circled the small herd carefully and closed in on them slowly. He stopped his mount and when Dan pulled up beside him Hawksley pointed to some of the steers.

'My brand,' he said. 'I expected this deal to go through,' he went on to explain, 'so I sent a couple of my men up north an' as soon as the rancher returned from Red Springs after settlin' with Mick he set some of his men on to help with the brandin'. I reckon they'd hev it finished by the time the rest of my outfit arrived an' it would save time when they got back to the Broken K.'

Dan nodded, and both men kicked their horses forward towards the Twisted M.

When Al Rockhill saw the sheriff approaching with Pete Hawksley he walked on to the verandah to meet them. They pulled to a halt in front of him and before Dan

101

realized what was happening Pete leaped from the saddle and grabbed Al by the shirt.

'I've a good mind to beat the daylights out of you,' snarled Pete angrily.

Al looked astonished. 'What am I supposed to hev done?' he snapped.

'Don't play innocent, you rustler,' snapped Pete.

'Rustler?' gasped Al as the sheriff pulled them apart.

'Hold it you two,' he snapped. 'Let's talk about this sensibly.'

'Sensibly?' snapped Pete. 'He doesn't understand sense; raidin' himself to try to throw suspicion on me.'

'Will someone tell me what this is all about?' asked Al.

Dan quickly explained what had happened. 'You're both tellin' the same story,' he finished. 'Now just ease off each other an' we might get somewhere.' He turned Pete towards his horse and forced him to mount and then swung on to his own mount.

'Cut your cattle out of my herd,' yelled Al, 'an' don't come round here with stupid ideas when you planted them there yourself to git at me.'

Anger darkened Pete's face at the accusation. He jerked his Colt from its holster but as he squeezed the trigger Dan, who had been watching Pete carefully as Al was speaking, pushed his horse hard against Pete's causing the animal to rear. The Colt roared but the bullet whined harmlessly into the air.

Rockhill crouched, his hand flying towards his holster. Dan, who skillfully kept his horse under control, drew his Colt in a flash.

'Leave it, Al!' he yelled.

Rockhill's hand froze on the butt of his Colt and Hawksley, who had steadied his horse, found himself faced with a Colt ready to swing on him if he made a false move.

'Put it back, Pete,' shouted Dan.

Slowly the owner of the Broken K slipped his Colt back into its holster.

'I'm not goin' to warn you again,' snapped Dan. 'This could flare into a range war an' I'm not goin' to have that. If there's any more trouble I'll clap you both in jail.' He paused a moment to let his words sink in. 'Now git out of here, Pete, Betty will be wondering where you are.'

Hawksley sullenly turned his horse and put it into a trot. Dan watched him for a few moments before looking at Rockhill.

'How many horses did you lose?' he asked.

'Ten,' came the brusque reply.

'Seven were used against the Broken K herd,' said Dan and kicked his horse into a trot leaving Rockhill guessing as to the meaning behind the words.

Chapter Seven

When Dan had sent Clint north to search the hills for trace of the masked gang he had instructed Clint to spend only two days away from the Red Springs as he wanted his deputy in town when he went to meet Lance Peters on the stage from Fort Worth.

Clint rode north at a steady pace which got the most out of the animal with the least effort so that its energy was conserved for any unforeseen circumstances. When he reached the hills he worked his way slowly westwards but saw no sign of any human being. As darkness began to envelop the countryside he chose a suitable place to camp, positioned so that his camp-fire would not betray his presence. He slept soundly and after an early breakfast continued his search westwards intending to swing southwards out of the hills about mid-afternoon and make his way back to Red Springs by nightfall.

Clint was beginning to despair of ever finding a clue when, about noon, he topped a rise, which led down to a valley, and suddenly turned his horse sharply back so that he was below the sky-line. He slipped quickly from the saddle, flattened himself on his stomach on the edge of the rise and peered cautiously into the valley. Below him a cowboy rode at a brisk trot seemingly bent on some special mission. Clint grunted with satisfaction at this stroke of luck. He hurried back to his horse, took his spyglass from his saddle-bag and returned to his vantage point. Training the glass on the cowboy he drew him into focus. A gasp of surprise and excitement escaped from his lips.

'Sol Evans of the Twisted M,' he whispered to himself.

He watched the cowboy pass below him and move further along the valley before he mounted his horse and followed. Clint kept well up the slope which afforded him a good view ahead but he could see nothing of the man's objective and it came as no surprise when Sol Evans turned his horse and climbed the slope at the far side of the valley. Clint halted his horse and waited until Evans had crossed the top of the slope before he followed. When he reached the top of the opposite hillside he saw that Evans was still proceeding at the same steady pace and

Clint regulated his speed to match that of the man ahead. They crossed a series of ridges before Evans rode carefully down a steep slope into a narrow twisting valley. When Clint was about halfway down the slope his horse dislodged some small stones which rolled and bounced down the hillside. Clint checked the animal and froze in the saddle tensed for action but Evans rode on oblivious to the clatter behind him.

When the noise subsided Clint breathed more freely, urged the horse forward and reached the bottom without further mishap. He turned after Evans and quickened his pace to close the gap between them in order to keep his quarry in sight through the twisting valley.

Too late he realized his mistake in not being more cautious for, when he rounded a bend, he found his path barred by three masked men on horseback each covering him with a Colt. He pulled to a halt, glanced round him but realized there was no way out. He was also aware that Sol Evans was not in sight.

'You haven't a chance if you touch that gun,' said one of the men. He nodded to his two companions who rode forward. One of them took Clint's Colt and rifle and before the deputy sheriff knew what was happening the other man brought the barrel of his Colt crashing on the back of Clint's head. Blackness swam in on him and he pitched from the saddle to sprawl unconscious on the hard ground.

Sol Evans moved from behind a group of rocks. 'Nice work, boys,' he praised with a grin. 'He's been followin' me fer some time, that's why I came in this way. I reckoned you'd figure somethin' was wrong when I crossed that last ridge.'

The four men were about to ride away when Evans halted them.

'Wait a minute,' he said. A smile creased his face as he felt in his pocket and pulled out a piece of paper and a stub of pencil. He marked the paper quickly and passed it to the masked men. 'I reckon the boss will appreciate that when we tell him.' The men glanced at the paper and chuckled when they saw what Evans had written. 'Stick it in his shirt,' said Evans and one of the men swung from his horse, rolled Clint over on to his back and tucked the piece of paper inside his shirt leaving half of it protruding so that the deputy sheriff could not miss it when he regained consciousness.

When he remounted his horse the four

men laughing raucously at their joke put their horses into a trot along the valley.

The sun beat down unmercifully on the unconscious figure and over an hour passed before Clint showed some sign of life. His eyes flickered open but quickly shut again against the glare of the blazing sun. Clint turned his throbbing head slowly and opened his eyes again. It took him a few moments to realize where he was then he struggled to sit up but his head spun and he flopped back his chest heaving as he gulped air into his lungs. His head cleared a little and a few minutes later Clint succeeded in sitting up. As he raised his hand to feel his head he saw the piece of paper protruding from his shirt. He pulled it out and his eyes widened when he read it. He was surprised at the audacity of the note and re-read it before stuffing it into his pocket. His head throbbed madly from the blow and the heat, and it pained him when he looked around. His sombrero lay a few yards away and his horse champed grass at the foot of the hill. Clint whistled softly. The horse tossed its head and pricked up its ears. Clint whistled again and this time the animal turned and with a low whinny walked towards him. When the horse reached him Clint smiled and spoke softly to it, before pushing himself to his feet. His head swam and he swayed, grasping his saddle for support. He waited a few moments summoning his strength then walked to his sombrero. The effort in bending to pick it up was almost too much for him, and when he straightened he was almost overcome by dizziness but the horse was beside him and he leaned against it to steady himself. When he put the sombrero on his head he felt immediate relief from the sun, and its wide brim stopped the glare from piercing his eyes. He looked round for his weapons and not seeing them guessed the masked men had taken them.

Clint turned to his horse, got one foot in the stirrup and grasping the saddle horn pulled himself into the leather. The effort took a lot of strength and he sat for a few minutes before sending the horse up the hillside in the direction of Red Springs.

What would normally have been a comparatively easy ride to him proved hard due to the effect of his wound and the sun, and it was almost dark when he reached town. He half-slipped and half-fell from the saddle when he halted in front of the sheriff's office. Staggering up the steps on to the sidewalk he fell against the door of the office which burst open under his weight as he turned the knob.

Dan McCoy and the Collins brothers were startled when Clint fell into the office. They were on their feet in a flash and helped their old friend into a chair.

'Get the doc, Jack,' said Dan sizing up the situation quickly.

Jack hurried from the office and Howard put some water on the stove in readiness for the doctor's arrival. Dan took a bottle of whisky from a cupboard and after pouring a long drink he forced some between Clint's parched lips. The old man coughed and spluttered but when Dan gave him another sip he felt the strong spirit driving feeling back into his body. He looked at Dan, relief showing in his eyes that he was back in the office and Dan realized that his deputy could have known little about his arrival in Red Springs.

Clint started to talk but Dan halted him. 'Jack's gone for the doc,' he said, 'save it until after he's seen you.'

It was not long before Jack and Doc Smith arrived and after the doctor had examined Clint he informed him that he would be all right but advised him to take things quietly for a couple of days. He dressed the wound and it was only after he had left that Dan would allow his deputy to talk.

Clint told his story quickly and, when he had finished, he pulled a piece of paper from his pocket.

'I found this tucked in my shirt,' he said. 'Those masked hombres must hev put it there.'

He handed the paper to Dan who glanced at it quickly and then read it aloud.

'Keep off my tail, lawman; I mean to git Mick Hawksley and his father for what has happened. Signed Al Rockhill!'

Jack and Howard gasped incredulously and stared wide-eyed at Dan with surprise.

'Then Rockhill is behind it all,' said Jack.

Dan rubbed his chin thoughtfully and sat down at his desk still staring at the note.

'Must be,' agreed Howard. 'This note an' the fact that Sol Evans was around when those masked men stopped Clint proves it.'

'Does it?' said Dan quickly.

The three men looked at Dan in amazement.

'But surely you don't think otherwise,' said Clint. 'I reckon you should git out to the Twisted M an' arrest him.'

'Do you figure a man would deliberately wreck his own ranch to throw suspicion on someone else?' said Dan.

'Might do if he was so desperate to cover up his crimes,' replied Howard.

'Don't forgit Rockhill said he had been prepared to await the outcome of the trial,' pointed out Dan. 'I know what you'll say,' he added quickly, 'a blind. You know this note could have been written by anyone.' He threw the note across the desk so Jack and Howard could see it. 'It has been printed so that we can't compare it with Al Rockhill's signature.'

Jack and Howard glanced at the paper and had to agree that it could have been the work of anyone.

'Well, how do you figure it?' asked Jack.

'I'm still thinkin' that there's some connection between this gang and the murder,' replied Dan. 'A third party had been in Mick's room, we know from that clay we found. I'm beginning to wonder if there's anyone who hates Rockhill and Hawksley enough to want to git at them both. I reckon it might be worth looking into but first I've got to meet Lance Peters tomorrow. Clint needs some rest so I'd like Jack and Howard to be here tomorrow; you never know if there might be another attempt to git at Mick. If you can dig up anything about Rockhill or

Hawksley that might help so much the better; I'll take it up when I've had a talk to Peters.'

The following day Dan McCoy left Red Springs along the east road before forking south-east in the direction of Mineral Wells where he intended to meet the stage from Fort Worth. He arrived in the small dusty town half an hour before the coach was due and, after taking his horse to the livery stables where he informed the owner he would call for his horse in a few days time, he carried his saddle to the stage office.

A lone cowboy rode slowly into town, swung from the saddle in front of the saloon and lounged against the rail. A short while later the pound of hoofs as the stage thundered into Mineral Wells brought Dan from the office and the man stiffened with surprise when he saw the lawman from Red Springs.

The driver of the stage handled his team well and pulling on the reins and using his foot on the brake-handle brought the coach to a halt in front of the office. He tied the reins quickly round the iron rail at his feet and jumped to the ground. He opened the stagecoach door and called out 'Twenty minutes stop, folks,' before turning to greet thc stage-line official in Mineral Wells and report an uneventful trip.

Dan moved forward as the passengers began to alight and he smiled a greeting at a tall, upright, well-built man of about thirty. The new arrival wore a black frock-coat, matching trousers and a black, wide-brimmed sombrero. A black string-tie was tied neatly at the collar of an immaculate white shirt.

'Hello, Lance,' greeted Dan extending his hand.

Lance Peters took Dan's hand in a firm grip. 'Glad to see you, Dan,' he smiled. 'How's Barbara?'

'Fine,' replied Dan. 'She's looking forward to seeing you. We've time for a drink,' he added and the two men walked along the sidewalk to the town's only saloon.

The cowboy who still leaned against the rail had watched them closely as they greeted each other but barely gave them a glance when they passed him and pushed their way through the batwings into the saloon.

Dan briefed Lance on the events in Red Springs so that none of the details would have to be discussed in front of the other three passengers on the stage. The lawyer listened intently as he sipped his whisky and looked thoughtful when Dan had finished. He was about to speak when the stage-line official looked over the top of the batwings and called out, 'Stage nearly ready to roll.' The two men finished their drinks and left the saloon unaware that a lone cowboy was greatly interested in their movements.

He cursed under his breath when he saw Dan come out of the office carrying his saddle, throw it up on to the top of the stage and follow Lance Peters into the coach. The cowboy shoved himself from the rail, swung on to his horse and rode out of Mineral Wells. Once clear of the town he kicked his horse into a gallop and headed north-west. He kept to a fast pace knowing that the stage coach would not be far behind. He avoided the small town of Graham and reckoned that the brief halt which the stage would make there would give him the extra time he wanted.

Half way between Graham and Red Springs the cowboy swung from the trail towards a group of low hills and as he approached them four horsemen appeared and rode to meet him. He pulled his horse to a sliding halt when he reached them.

'Is he on it, Greg?' asked one of the men who was obviously the leader.

'Sure he is, Ace,' answered Greg as he gasped for breath after the hard ride. 'But so is McCoy from Red Springs!'

'What!' gasped Ace.

Greg quickly explained what he had seen in Mineral Wells and when he had finished Ace grinned.

'Wal,' he said, 'if McCoy hasn't got his horse I figure he doesn't suspect anythin', he'd hev ridden behind the coach if he had expected trouble. We'll give that lawman a mighty big surprise. C'm on.'

He kicked his horse forward followed by the other men and before long they had taken up their positions at a point where the trail swung through a cutting in the group of low hills.

As the stage coach swung and bounced along the trail out of Mineral Wells Lance Peters whispered quietly to Dan McCoy.

'From what you've told me things look black for Mick Hawksley,' he said. 'There is strong evidence against him but I'll try and work on this idea of yours that someone else was in the room. I might just conceivably put some doubt in the minds of the jury; if so they could bring in a verdict of insufficient evidence, but it's a slim chance.' He paused thoughtfully. 'Do you think there's any likelihood of finding a link, between this gang and the murder?' he asked.

'We haven't turned anything up yet,' replied Dan. 'It didn't seem like it at first but I'm not so sure now; maybe somebody's trying to get at Hawksley and Rockhill. We're working on that angle now.'

'Let's hope you turn something up,' said Peters. 'Mick's life may depend on it!'

The stage-coach kept good time and after a brief stop in Graham rolled again on schedule. The driver and shot-gun swayed and sweated under the afternoon sun and looked forward to reaching Red Springs after another uneventful run. The trail swung away from the east bank of the Brazo to take the easiest way through a group of low hills. The driver eased the speed a little as the gradient fell slightly to a narrow cutting. As they rounded a bend he was startled to see three masked horsemen barring their path. For a split second the driver was tempted to lash his team of six horses into a gallop to try to break through and, in the same instance, the shot-gun started to raise his rifle but a warning shot over their heads made them see the hopelessness of the situation. The shotgun lowered his rifle and the driver hauled on the reins to bring his tcam to a halt.

The crash of a gun coupled with the sudden slowing down of the coach startled the passengers. Dan glanced out of the window and stiffened when he saw a masked rider, with Colt drawn, swing alongside the coach. He started to reach for his gun but a warning shot from the other side of the coach made him turn to see another masked man already close to the coach covering the passengers with his weapon. The wheels ground to a halt and almost immediately the coach door was flung open and the passengers ordered out at the point of a gun by a sixth man.

As they clambered out Dan's mind raced. This was a new area for the masked men; were they gradually moving southwards? If so then his theories that the gang might be connected with Kathy's murder had no foundation. Dan shuffled alongside Lance as the passengers lined up and the driver and shot-gun jumped down from their seat.

'This the gang you were telling me about?' whispered Lance.

'Reckon so,' replied Dan but he had no time to say any more for the man who had opened the door now relieved them of their weapons.

A tall man on a black horse rode nearer to them. 'Just behave yourselves an' no one will git hurt,' he told them in a deep voice. 'We hev no quarrel with anyone but we want you,' he added pointing at Lance Peters.

The lawyer looked startled and looked at Dan who was equally surprised but quickly composed himself and with an almost imperceptible nod indicated to Peters to do as he was told. Dan's thoughts raced. Why pick on Lance Peters unless this gang was connected with Kathy's killing. This seemed to prove that they were. He was puzzled. One of the riders came up leading a horse and Lance Peters was pushed forward towards it.

'Mount up,' ordered the leader. 'An' no tricks. I should hate to put a bullet in you. We just want you out of the way until after the trial.'

Dan stiffened and almost gasped when the leader's horse half turned and he saw the Twisted M brand. Rockhill must be behind this; he was keeping Mick's lawyer out of the way; who else would want to do this but Rockhill? Dan glanced round desperately but saw it was useless to try anything; they were covered by too many guns.

Reluctantly Lance Peters shuffled forward and mounted the horse. As soon as he was in the saddle and the sixth man was mounted the gang turned their horses and kicked them into a gallop away from the scene of the hold up.

Dan watched them go thoughtfully and when they disappeared into the hills he was suddenly galvanized into action.

'Everyone on board, quick,' he shouted at the group of people who were talking and wondering what it was all about. 'Driver,' he called, 'Red Springs in the fastest time you've ever done!'

Chapter Eight

Pete Hawksley stood outside the stage office awaiting the arrival of the stage from Fort Worth. He planned to take Lance Peters to meet his son as soon as he arrived. He knew that Dan McCoy would have told the lawyer everything but he was anxious that Peters should meet Mick as soon as possible.

Hawksley glanced impatiently at his pocket watch, wishing the minutes away; a quarter of an hour before the stage was due he looked up; was he mistaken or had he heard the noise of hoofs? He listened intently looking along the main street. Excitement seized him; he was not mistaken. The pound of hoofs had grown more distinct; the stage was early! He watched anxiously as the noise grew louder and then the stage tore round the corner into the main street. The coach swayed and rocked as the driver urged his team onwards. Hawksley was startled; the stage never hit the main street at this speed and when it showed no sign of slowing down for the stage office he realized something was wrong. Alarm showed on his face when the coach thundered past and only started to lose speed as it neared the sheriff's office. He started to run and several other people on the street did likewise. The stage official tore out of his office and was alongside Hawksley sprinting down the street. The driver hauled hard on the reins and clamped on the brake to bring the coach to a sliding, swaying halt outside the sheriff's office. Curious townsfolk clustered round as the driver jumped down yelling that there had been a hold-up.

Pete Hawksley reached the coach as Dan jumped out. 'What's happened?' he panted grasping Dan by the arm.

'Come inside, Pete,' he said and pushed his way through the gathering crowd to his office followed by the rancher.

Jack and Howard Collins had already appeared at the door and as Dan and Pete hurried inside they followed them and closed the door.

'Where's Peters?' gasped Hawksley alarm and concern showing in his voice.

'Kidnapped!' replied Dan.

'What!' the three men gasped together.

Dan quickly related what had happened.

'Rockhill's gone too far this time!' snarled Hawksley his face dark with anger. His voice fell to a whisper and his eyes filled with hate. 'I'll git him fer this,' he hissed and swung to the door.

Dan jumped in front of him and grasped him by the shoulders. 'Hold it, Pete!' he snapped. 'Cool off before you leave here otherwise you'll be doin' somethin' you'll regret.'

Hawksley looked at Dan in amazement. 'You aren't lettin' him git away with this?' he gasped.

'Someone will answer for it,' replied Dan quietly.

Hawksley looked somewhat disgusted as he shook himself free of Dan's grip. 'Someone?' he snapped. 'This is Rockhill's work it's as plain as a pikestaff. I hire a lawyer, the best, a man known to you, you announce he's been kidnapped, there's only one man who wouldn't want him to get here – Rockhill, the same man who tried to lynch Mick, you saw that with your own eyes. Then he hit my cattle – the brand was on the horses used by the raiders, same brand as you say was on those used by the kidnappers. What more do you want? And if you don't do somethin' about Rockhill, I will!'

'Nobody kidnaps a man from under my nose and gets away with it,' replied Dan coldly. 'All I want is for you not to make a fool of yourself.'

'But they were Rockhill's horses,' put in Howard Collins.

'That's just the point,' answered Dan. 'These masked raiders rustled some horses from the Twisted M. I know you'll say that was a blind organised by Rockhill to throw suspicion from himself,' he hastened to add when he saw Hawksley start to protest, 'but I don't believe a man would go to the length of wrecking his own home.'

'What about the attempted lynchin'?' snapped Hawksley.

'That was genuine enough,' agreed Dan. 'But it was done immediately after the murder in a fit of temper. I believe Rockhill regretted it afterwards.'

'Rubbish,' stormed Hawksley. 'That man would go to any length to git at Mick and me.'

Dan saw it would be useless to try to reason further with the rancher. 'I'll certainly question Rockhill,' he said. 'Get me a horse, Jack.'

'I'm comin' with you,' said Hawksley. 'Rockhill isn't wriggling out of this one. I want Peters to be here to defend my son.'

Jack soon returned with a horse and the

sheriff and the rancher left Red Springs at a brisk pace in the direction of the Twisted M.

As they neared the ranch Dan detected a certain tenseness and uneasiness in the man at his side and when Rockhill appeared on the verandah of the ranch-house he saw Hawksley stiffen in the saddle. Dan edged his horse closer to Hawksley as they pulled to a halt in front of the house.

'You two again,' greeted Rockhill. 'What hev I done this time?'

'You know!' snapped Hawksley and suddenly jerked his Colt from its holster.

Dan, who had been suspicious of Hawksley's attitude, flung himself from his saddle almost before the gun had left leather. His shoulder crashed into Hawksley's side and at the same time he knocked the rancher's arm upwards. The Colt roared but the bullet whined harmlessly into the roof of the house. The weight and suddenness of the impact knocked Hawksley from the saddle and the two men fell to the hard ground. The breath was driven from Hawksley's body but Dan twisted and was on his feet in a flash standing over the man on the ground.

Rockhill was surprised by the unexpectedness and speed of the events but even so a Colt appeared in his hand by the time Dan was on his feet. The sheriff glanced sharply at the owner of the Twisted M who crouched ready for anything.

'Put that away,' snapped Dan. He stepped to one side, picked up Hawksley's Colt and quickly emptied the chamber.

As Hawksley climbed to his feet, annoyance clearly marked on his face, Rockhill reluctantly slipped his Colt back into its holster.

'You've almost gone too far, Pete,' snapped Dan angrily. 'My patience is almost at its limit. I'm the law around here and things will be done my way!' He handed the empty gun to Hawksley who took it without a word. Dan turned to Rockhill. 'Know anything about the kidnappin' of a lawyer from the stage from Fort Worth?' he asked.

Rockhill looked surprised. 'Nothing,' he answered firmly.

'Horses bearing your brand were used!' said Dan, watching Rockhill's reactions carefully.

The rancher gasped. 'I know nothing about it!' he said.

'You're a liar,' snapped Hawksley.

'Shut up!' snarled Dan.

'Don't forget I've had some horses rustled,' put in Rockhill. 'Reckon it could hev been Hawksley here usin' those horses to throw suspicion on me.'

Dan glared angrily at the two men. 'I'm tired of you two accusing each other,' he snapped. 'I've explained to Hawksley why I don't think it was you an' now I'll tell you why I don't think it was Hawksley. The man that was kidnapped was comin' to defend Mick Hawksley an' it's not likely that Pete would kidnap him.' Both men remained silent under the lash of Dan's tongue. 'By your bickering at each other you're wasting my time trying to keep you both from running into trouble and doin' something you'd regret fer the rest of your lives. There's not long to the trial an' there's a lot I've got to do, so keep apart an' cause no more trouble otherwise you'll end up in jail until the trial.' Both men looked sheepish under Dan's admonishment. Neither of them spoke. The sheriff looked hard at Hawksley. 'Mount up, Pete an' ride; I've somethin' else I want to ask Al.'

Hawksley turned, walked slowly to his horse, swung into the saddle and without a backward glance rode away from the Twisted M.

Dan watched him for a few moments before turning to Rockhill. 'What do you know about Sol Evans?'

'Sol Evans!' Rockhill looked surprised at the question. 'What for?'

'That's my affair,' replied Dan and waited for Rockhill to answer his question.

After a moment's thought the rancher replied. 'There's not much I can tell you. He came to me about a year ago lookin' fer a job. I gave him a fortnight's trial; he measured up to my standards so I took him on. I ask no questions; if a man is good at his job that's all I ask; his past is of no importance to me. I don't even know where Evans came from.'

Dan rubbed his chin thoughtfully then suddenly with a curt 'Thanks' he spun on his heel and hurried to his horse leaving a surprised man staring after him.

When Dan McCoy reached his office in Red Springs he found Clint Schofield and the Collins brothers awaiting his return.

'Any luck?' asked Clint eagerly.

Dan shook his head as he threw his Stetson on to his desk and sat down wearily in his chair. 'Rockhill denied any knowledge of the kidnapping,' he said and went on to relate the happenings at the Twisted M.

'It certainly looks as if you're right, Dan,' said Jack when Dan had expressed his ideas. 'There must be a third party hitting at

130

Hawksley and Rockhill but I can't see any connection between the murder and these masked men.'

'That's what puzzles me,' replied Dan, 'an' yet I hev a feeling' that Mick is tellin' the truth an' there was someone else in the room but how this gang is connected I can't see.'

'There must be some connection,' muttered Clint. 'These raids didn't begin until after the murder; surely it can't be coincidence thet the two families linked in the murder hev been raided.'

'I reckon there's someone playing on the fact that Hawksley an' Rockhill hev been thrown into conflict,' said Howard. 'Maybe even committed the murder to precipitate that.'

'But that means a common enemy,' pointed out Jack.

'You might hev somethin' there,' said Dan.

'Let's see what we know about the two families,' suggested Howard.

'Wal, Hawksleys are an old established family around here,' pointed out Clint. 'Rockhill's the newcomer.'

'Came here from Gainesville about five years ago,' mused Dan. 'Was lookin' fer a new home an' Hawksley withdrew his offer for the Twisted M to let Rockhill have it.

They've been firm friends ever since until this trouble. Anyone know anything about Rockhill's past?'

The three men shook their heads.

'Never heard it mentioned,' said Clint.

Dan's eyes brightened. 'Then I figure it might be worth lookin' into,' he said. 'I'll ride to Gainesville in the morning. However, we must get a lead on Lance Peters. We know this gang hev got him an' are holed up in the hills; we also know that Sol Evans has some connection with them so I reckon our best chance of makin' contact is through him. Jack, Howard, I'd like you to keep a watch on the Twisted M an' see what Evans gits up to.' The two men nodded. 'Clint,' added Dan turning to his deputy, 'I'd like you to keep watch on Mick, you never know if there may be another attempt to git him. Swear in any more deputies if you think it necessary. I'll be back as soon as possible.'

The four men talked for another hour and it was dark when Dan and the Collins brothers left the office. Clint locked up after them and settled down for the night.

About the same time as Clint turned the key in the office door two shadowy figures emerged from the darkness and rode towards each other in a small hollow half way between the Broken K and Twisted M ranches. They pulled their horses to a halt alongside each other and exchanged greetings.

'Things are goin' well,' said one of them, a note of authority and satisfaction in his voice. 'The boys did good work to git Peters from under the sheriff's nose. If anyone could hev got young Hawksley off it would have been Peters. We've got to keep him out of the way until after the trial; Mick's sure to git the rope, then Hawksley an' Rockhill will be at each others throats.' There was a pleasurable gloating in his voice as his thoughts raced. 'I reckon Sheriff McCoy might git a bit nosy after the kidnappin' so I figure we should keep an eye on him. Ride to the hills an' tell Jamie to git into town before daylight an' tail McCoy wherever he goes an' take whatever action he thinks necessary.'

Sol Evans muttered his understanding and kicked his horse forward up the slight slope. The other man watched him go, then, satisfied that his plans were going well, he turned his horse and rode out of the hollow.

The following morning after Dan had bid his wife farewell he rode to his office, checked that everything was all right with

133

Clint, and took the east road out of town unaware that the man who had watched him in Fort Worth had climbed into the saddle in front of the saloon and was now following him in the direction of Gainesville.

Jamie matched his pace to that of the sheriff's, keeping well back so that he would not be conspicuous. As morning passed beyond noon Jamie was a little perturbed; the sheriff's ride was taking an unexpected direction. He eased himself in the saddle and kept his horse at the steady pace they had been travelling all morning. About mid-afternoon Jamie saw a town appear on the horizon and, as they neared it, he shortened the distance between himself and the man ahead. When he rode into the main street of Gainesville he saw McCoy swinging from the saddle in front of the sheriff's office. Jamie frowned, realizing there was nothing he could do but wait until McCoy re-appeared. He pulled his horse amongst some others tied to the rail in front of the saloon and, mounting the sidewalk, leaned on the rail and rolled himself a cigarette.

After Dan had introduced himself to the Sheriff of Gainesville he came straight to the point. 'I'm checkin' on a man named Rock-hill,' he said. 'I believe he used to live here, left about five years ago.'

The Gainesville man looked thoughtful then shook his head slowly. 'I don't know of anyone by that name,' he replied, 'but then I've only been here two years.'

Dan looked a little dismayed. He had been hopeful that the answer to his problems lay in Rockhill's past life at Gainesville. 'You never heard anyone talk about him?' he asked.

The sheriff shook his head. 'No, can't say I recall the name at all. Are you sure he came from here?'

'Wal, that isn't certain,' answered Dan, 'but I'd heard so.'

'Sorry I can't help you,' said the lawman, 'but I'll tell you what to do, visit old Lee behind the bar in the saloon; he's spent most of his life here and should be able to tell you if anyone by the name of Rockhill lived here.'

'Thanks,' said Dan. 'I was figurin' on stayin' the night so that'll fit in well. Thanks fer your help.' He left the sheriff's office, untied his horse from the rail and rode to the livery stables unaware that a cowboy was watching his movements.

When he saw Dan approaching the livery stable Jamie untied his horse and moved slowly in the same direction, holding back until Dan reappeared carrying his saddle-bags. Jamie stopped outside the stables until he saw Dan turn into the hotel then he led his horse inside and a few moments later came back on to the street and hurried to the hotel. He guessed Dan had decided to stay the night and as he signed the register, booking himself a room, he saw Dan's signature immediately above his. Jamie hurried to his room, had a quick wash and returned to the lobby where he deposited himself in a chair and made a pretence of reading the Gainesville Chronicle. He was not sorry when Dan reappeared half an hour later and strolled across the street to the café. Jamie enjoyed his meal and when Dan left the café he followed him to the town's only saloon.

Dan crossed to the bar and Jamie strolled across to lean on the counter beside him. He took no notice of the Sheriff of Red Springs and when he had got his drink he half turned his back to him.

Dan finished his drink and called for another. When the old man placed the glass in front of him Dan watched him carefully weighing up the right approach to make.

'Hev a drink on me, Lee,' said Dan.

The old barman looked startled at the

mention of his name. He rubbed his greying moustache a little nervously.

'Thanks, stranger,' he muttered. 'How do you know my name?'

Dan thought a little flattery would not go amiss. 'The barman of Gainesville has quite a reputation,' he said and saw a gleam of pride come into the old man's eyes. 'Heard you'd seen some rip-roaring times when this was a wild frontier,' he added. 'Thought you might be able to help me, an' your sheriff confirmed this opinion.'

The old man poured himself a whisky. 'Your health, stranger,' he said. 'What old Lee hasn't seen out here is worth forgettin'!'

'Then I figure I've found the right man,' said Dan. 'I'm trying to trace a man called Rockhill; heard he lived here, probably about five years ago.'

The old man rubbed his moustache thoughtfully. 'Wal,' he drawled, 'I've been around here fer close on forty years but I can't say as how I ever heard of that name.'

Despair flooded into Dan's mind. He had drawn a blank. 'You certain?' he asked. 'I was told he'd left here about five years ago.'

'Son,' said the old man, 'I've a good memory especially fer people an' pride myself on being able to name all the folks that hev

137

lived in these parts in my time. No, nobody by the name of Rockhill lived round here. Only person to leave Gainesville five years ago was a man by the name of Richards; he an' his daughter.'

Dan gasped; excitement filled him; his thoughts raced. He cursed himself; why hadn't he thought of it before? He had taken it for granted that Rockhill was Al's real name; of course a man could lose himself in the west under an assumed name.

'What was this Richards like?' asked Dan eagerly.

'Wal,' drawled the barman trying to re-capture a picture of the man he knew as Richards, 'he was a big man, powerfully built an' that power seemed to flow from him making him a dominant personality. He had fair hair an' grey eyes. His wife was a charming person, seemed to mellow the man; she died about ten years back. Richards took it bad and he seemed to harden after that, but he had a love an' deep affection fer his only child, a girl.' He paused, rubbing his chin, 'Let me see, what was her name – Kathy that was it, Kathy, she'd be about eighteen when they left here.'

Dan almost shouted with joy. The description fitted; he felt he was getting somewhere. He picked up the bottle of whisky and poured another drink for the old man who muttered his thanks. He had warmed to his subject and Dan pressed it further.

'I'm rather anxious to git in touch with him,' he said. 'Know where he went?'

Lee shook his head. 'Sorry, I don't,' he replied. 'Richards left without a word to anyone. Mind you it was only what we expected after what happened.'

'What was that?' asked Dan eagerly, feeling he was on the point of gaining some knowledge which would throw light on the recent happenings in Red Springs.

'Richards owned quite a sizeable spread east of town,' explained Lee. 'A tract of land with some valuable water rights on it came up fer sale. A man by the name of Wilson owned a small spread to the north of thet land; it was always touch an' go fer him in dry weather but with that land he'd be all right. The land wasn't essential to Richards but I must say that with it the value of his spread increased enormously. Wal, Richards outbid Wilson.' He paused to sip his whisky. Dan waited anxiously for the old man to continue. Lee put down his glass and stared at it thoughtfully. 'You know,' he said, 'if Richards' wife had still been alive at the time

I don't think anythin' would hev happened. I believe she would hev persuaded him to let Wilson have it. Everyone else around here was of the same opinion. Richards had hardened and all he could see was making everythin' as secure as possible for his daughter; I'm afraid that feelin' blinded him to lots of things.'

'So Richards made an enemy out of Wilson,' said Dan as Lee picked up his glass again.

'No,' replied Lee to Dan's astonishment for now he thought he had a reason for someone to want to get at Rockhill as he knew him.

'But I…' began Dan.

'Everythin' was fair an' square,' explained Lee, 'don't get me wrong; Richards didn't try any dirty work he jest out-bid Wilson. Wilson was a peaceable man an' he jest resigned himself to meeting the tough times of dry weather again.' The bartender stopped when two cowboys called for some drinks and Dan waited anxiously, hoping that the old man would not cool to his story. A few minutes later Lee returned and much to Dan's relief had not to be pressed to continue his tale. 'The crisis didn't come with the sale of that land, it came a year later. We were hit by the worst drought we'd had for a very long time.

140

Everyone was hit in some way or other but Wilson could do nothin', he stood there an' hed to watch his cattle die; he was ruined. It was too much fer him; everythin' he'd built up was gone an' he committed suicide. His wife found him hangin' in a barn an' the shock killed her.'

'Did this cause Richards to leave?' asked Dan.

'Indirectly,' replied Lee. 'Wilson had a son, Ben, about eighteen, the same age as Kathy; they'd been seen around together, then fer some reason she'd snubbed him. I think Ben took it too much to heart an' maybe, with thet smouldering inside him when this tragedy happened, he blamed Richards fer the deaths of his parents. He talked hard an' hot against Richards, said if Richards hadn't got thet land his father wouldn't hev been ruined. I suppose there was truth in what he said but you know, if we took everything to those sort of conclusions everyone would be hating everyone else. However, he stirred up a lot of feelin' against Richards, not thet any folk around here took any positive action but there was a tension which became rather unbearable. Then, one night Ben Wilson hed been drinkin' hard; he went out to Richards' ranch an' tried to kill Richards. Fortunately

141

he failed but of course was tried fer attempted murder an' I figure he was lucky to git off with a two year sentence.'

'An' it was after this thet Richards left?'

The old man nodded. 'Whether he was afraid for himself or Kathy I don't know; you see Ben Wilson was led from the trial screaming vengeance on Richards and his daughter. Richards sold up an' he an' Kathy left without tellin' anyone where they were goin'.'

'What was this Ben Wilson like?' asked Dan.

'An ordinary sort of bloke,' replied Lee. 'Nothin' really distinguishable about him unless it be his shaggy eyebrows. Mind you he'd altered a lot when he came out of prison. He'd aged beyond his years an' hed the look of a man who'd nursed a hate every second of his time behind bars.'

'You saw him again?' said Dan.

'Sure, he came back here, looking fer Richards but no one could help him an' I don't suppose they would hev if they could, not with the hate thet was in him,' replied Lee.

'What happened to him?' questioned Dan.

'Don't know,' answered Lee. 'He drifted away from here, in fact his goin' away probably did the town a blessin'; some no good hoodlums went with him. Reckon thet lot could easily hev gone wrong. A pity,' he muttered, 'fer there was somethin' about Ben Wilson that I liked an' I've seen some men handle horses in my time but Ben Wilson stood with the best of them even at eighteen.'

'That's a mighty interestin' story,' said Dan, 'but I'm afraid it brings me no nearer findin' Richards or rather Rockhill as I know him, that is if it's the same man.'

'Sorry, son, I can't help you any more, when Richards left Gainesville he vanished from the face of the earth,' said Lee.

Dan drew two silver dollars from his pocket and passed them to the old man thanking him for his trouble. He turned and left the saloon unaware that the man at the bar beside him had been interested in how much information the Sheriff from Red Springs was able to gain.

Dan returned to the hotel knowing full well that Rockhill was the Richards of the story and that he had found someone who wanted revenge but he was still puzzled as to where Hawksley fitted into the picture. As he climbed into bed Dan's mind was on Ben Wilson. He knew no one of that name

143

and the only two significant things about him were shaggy eyebrows and an ability to handle horses. Dan knew it was little to go on and he could think of no one who fitted this slight description, and yet something nagged at the back of his mind. He fell asleep pleased that he had made the trip to Gainesville.

In the next room Jamie climbed into bed, plans already formulated for the following day.

When Dan left the hotel the next morning the man in the adjacent room had already left and was seated at a table against the window in the café from which he could see the hotel. Jamie guessed that with the information Dan had gained it would not be long before he returned to Red Springs, he had something to work on. Jamie had his horse tied to the rail outside the café and when Dan appeared and crossed to the café Jamie lingered over his breakfast. McCoy seemed eager to be on his way and after a quick breakfast hurried to the livery stable. Jamie watched him from the café and, when he saw Dan leave Gainesville by the west road he paid his bill and was soon in the saddle. He took a side road out of town and cut across country at a fast gallop until he reached the trail some distance ahead of Dan.

Although eager to reach Red Springs Dan kept his horse to a steady pace to conserve both his energy and that of the animal as the sun beat fiercely down over the Texas countryside.

He had been riding about two hours, relaxed in the saddle, turning over his problems in his mind, when he approached a boulder-strewn dip in the trail. Suddenly he stiffened and almost instantaneously flung himself from the saddle. A glint of light had caught his eye and as he moved a rifle crashed. A searing pain jerked through his shoulder as the bullet penetrated deeply. He hit the ground hard, rolled over and lay still, thankful that the would-be killer had overlooked the reflection of the sun on his rifle otherwise he would have been a dead man now. Dan's brain pounded, and in spite of the pain in his shoulder, kept still, watching for the appearance of the man behind the rifle in case he should come to make sure of his kill. His wound was bleeding freely and Dan realized he would have to do something soon. The long minutes passed and as no one had appeared Dan decided that the man must have gone. He reached for his Stetson which had fallen beside him, and pushed himself slowly to his feet. His head swam and he almost fell again, but he summoned his strength and staggered to his horse. He supported himself against the side of the animal and after resting there for a few moments struggled to pull himself into the saddle. His third attempt was successful and he flopped into the leather, sagging forward over the saddle-horn. Although he felt sapped of energy he knew he must be moving and he tapped his horse with his heels sending the animal forward at a walk. Dan relaxed in the saddle and in spite of the pain from his shoulder he felt some of his strength returning.

As the animal followed the trail through the upheaval of boulders to the grassland Dan turned his attention to his wound and managed to staunch the flow of blood with his neckerchief. He realized however, that he must seek attention soon and once on the undulating grassland he shaded his eyes against the glare and searched for sign of a ranch-house. A quarter of an hour passed before Dan noticed a break in the horizon and turned his horse towards it. Drawing nearer he was relieved to see a house and before long the rancher and two of his men ran out to meet him. They helped him from his horse and took him inside the house where the rancher, aided by his wife, speedily and efficiently dressed Dan's wound. Fortunately the bullet had passed right through the fleshy part of the shoulder and once he had received attention and had enjoyed a meal Dan felt stronger. The rancher tried to persuade him to stay the night but Dan felt he should get back to Red Springs.

He thanked the rancher and his wife and took his leave of them. He regretted the delay which had been caused but wisely kept to a steady pace which would not tax his strength. As he rode he turned events over in his mind, wondering who had tried to kill him and why. Dan realized it must be connected with this trip and yet only his wife, Clint, Jack and Howard knew the reason for his visit to Gainesville. They were all absolutely trustworthy and Dan came to the conclusion that someone had been watching him. The sheriff settled himself more easily in the saddle pleased with his conclusion for it meant someone was frightened and a frightened man could easily make a slip!

Chapter Nine

As Dan McCoy was riding to Gainesville Jack and Howard Collins headed for the Twisted M. They took up an advantageous position and taking it in turns to use the spy-glass, they noted every movement, but Sol Evans did not leave the ranch. When darkness fell they secured their horses and crept closer to the buildings.

An hour passed before a shaft of light pierced the darkness as the door of the bunk-house was opened. A shadowy figure stepped out, closed the door behind him and paused before moving in the direction of the stable.

'Could be him,' whispered Jack. 'I'll take a closer look.'

He slipped quietly away from his brother and crouching low hurried forward towards the buildings. Reaching a fence he paused, listening intently, but all was quiet and the man was still in the stable. His eyes swept across the buildings but there was no movement. Jack climbed between the cross-rails of the fence and sprinted swiftly and silently to the space between the stable and the bunk-house. He flattened himself in the shadows against the side of the stable close to the corner. He tensed himself, listening for some sound from the stable. A few minutes later he heard the tread of quiet footsteps and the soft clop of hoofs. The sound stopped momentarily then started again becoming a little louder and Jack guessed the man had emerged from the stable pausing to make sure no one was about.

Excitement seized Jack. Why should a man steal quietly away from the ranch? Jack inched his way forward and peered cautiously round the corner of the building. He was only just in time to catch a glimpse of the man's face as he turned away from him. Sol Evans! Jack watched him leading the horse until both man and animal were lost in the darkness.

Jack raced for the fence, scrambled quickly through the rails and was soon beside Howard.

'Sol Evans,' he whispered urgently. 'C'm on!'

The two men hurried to their horses and moved quickly across the grassland to come on to the trail taken by Evans a short distance from the ranch.

'Hope he hasn't cut off,' whispered Jack anxiously.

They moved forward as quickly as they dare and were relieved when they saw a shadowy figure ahead. Suddenly Evans stopped and Jack and Howard froze in their tracks. The Twisted M man swung into his saddle and when he started to ride on the brothers climbed on their horses and followed. After riding a short distance Evans left the trail and cut across the range.

'Headin' for the Broken K!' whispered Howard.

Evans kept to a gentle pace and as the moon began to come up Jack and Howard dropped further behind, so as not to be conspicuous. About half way between the two ranches Evans disappeared from sight over a dip in the land. The Collins brothers approached the dip cautiously and halted a few yards from it. Howard slipped from his horse, moved forward stealthily, expecting to be able to wave his brother forward. He reached the edge of the incline and suddenly dropped to his stomach. Sol Evans was waiting in the hollow! Howard watched but the man showed no inclination to move on. He was still astride his horse and as far as

Howard could make out appeared to have reached the end of his ride. He was puzzled as he tried to find a reason. Suddenly he edged back from the hollow, jumped to his feet and ran to Jack who was getting a little uneasy.

'He's in the hollow,' said Howard. 'Reckon he's waitin' fer someone.'

'This might give us our lead,' said Jack eagerly.

'I figure if we work round to the right,' said Howard, 'we'll git a better view. One of us can watch whilst the other looks after our horses, we might need them in a hurry.'

The two men moved to the right until they were in the position Howard thought best. They slipped from the saddles and whilst Jack stayed with the horses Howard crept carefully to the hollow. Evans was still seated on his horse but was still alone. Howard listened carefully, straining to pick up the sound of an approaching horse but nothing stirred in the silent countryside. Ten minutes passed then Evans pulled his horse round and rode out of the hollow, taking the path by which he had come.

Howard, disappointed, pushed himself to his feet. What had been the purpose of this trip? He had felt sure Evans was going to meet someone in this hollow. He hurried to Jack.

'What happened?' asked his brother.

'Nothing,' replied Howard.

'What!' Jack was amazed. 'No one turn up?'

'No,' said Howard.

'Where's Sol now?' asked Jack.

'Appears to be heading back to the Twisted M,' replied Howard.

'C'm on, we'd better keep him in sight,' said Jack.

The two men swung into the saddles and turned their horses after Evans. It was an uneventful journey and the brothers watched Evans dismount a short distance from the ranch, lead his horse cautiously to the stable and then return to the bunk-house.

'Guess he won't wander again tonight,' observed Jack an hour later. 'I reckon we can make camp.'

The brothers moved to the shelter of a group of hillocks a short distance from the ranch and settled down for the night.

'What do you make of it?' asked Jack as they sipped some coffee.

'I figure Evans expected to meet some-one,' answered Howard thoughtfully. 'Either that person was unable to keep the rendez-vous or this has been a regular meeting to pass on messages and maybe there was nothing to report tonight.'

'Wal, your second theory could be right so if we keep a close watch on Evans we'll git our answer sooner or later.'

'An' if he's the link between someone an' the gang in the hills then he'll lead us to them eventually,' mused Jack. 'I reckon we might be close to learning the truth. Wonder if Dan has found anythin' out in Gaines-ville.'

Jack and Howard were awake before day-break and after a quick breakfast resumed their watch on the Twisted M. There was great activity around the buildings and it was not long before all the cowboys, with the exception of three, were mounted. Al Rockhill came out of his house, spoke to the foreman who then led the cowboys out on to the range.

'It looks as if Evans is stayin' behind,' observed Howard.

'Thank goodness fer that,' said Jack. 'It will be easier to keep an eye on him here.'

They saw Rockhill speak to two of his men who entered one of the buildings, emerged a few minutes later with various tools and proceeded to some broken fencing a short distance from the ranch-house. Rockhill watched them go before turning to Evans. He spoke to him for about five minutes then the two men went to the stables. The ranch owner came out with a horse, swung into the saddle, and rode after his outfit across the range. Evans walked to a corral where there were five horses. He cut one out into the neighbouring corral and started working on it to break it into a useful saddle-horse. The morning passed and at noon the three Twisted M cowboys broke off from their work for a meal. An hour later Evans was back in the corral starting work on the third horse. He had some difficulty cutting it out from the others and after doing so he found it resented his approach.

Suddenly Howard shook Jack who had been dozing. 'Burt Weldon ridin' past,' he said and handed the spy-glass to his brother.

Jack focused the spy-glass on the rider. 'Don't see what he has to do with Evans,' he said.

Weldon stopped his horse and sat watching Evans at work with the horse. A few minutes later he rode slowly to the corral and swung from the saddle on to the top rail of the fence. He sat for a moment then he jumped down, walked towards Evans and spoke to him before moving cautiously forward towards the horse. The animal shied and reared with a frightened whinney but gradually it settled down becalmed by the gentle voice. Weldon reached backwards without taking his eyes off the horse. Evans handed him a bridle to which was attached a long rein. Talking soothingly to the horse Weldon slipped the bridle over the horse's head with very little protestation from the animal. He gave the horse a friendly pat before gradually working his way slowly backwards along the length of rein to the centre of the corral. He worked the horse round the corral several times, before handing over to a smiling Evans. Weldon gave him a friendly slap on the shoulder, strolled to the fence, climbed over, mounted his horse and rode slowly away.

'He sure handled thet horse,' remarked Howard Collins, admiration showing in his voice. 'It was giving Evans a rough time up to then.'

'Looks as if we aren't goin' to see much happen today,' said Jack as he settled down again. 'Guess there'll be another night ride.'

Ten minutes passed and Howard shook Jack again. Evans walked across to the stable. He appeared a few moments later with his horse, shouted something to the two men repairing the fence, and then rode away from the ranch at a brisk trot.

Howard and Jack scrambled to their feet and hurried to their horses. Once in the saddles they quickly circled to the trail behind Evans and were surprised to see him lashing his horse in a fast gallop across the grassland.

'C'm on,' yelled Jack. 'He's headin' for the hills an' it looks mighty urgent.'

The two men kicked their mounts forward. The horses stretched themselves into a gallop and with Evans already a good way ahead the brothers had a hard ride to keep him in sight without being seen and also to close the gap before reaching the hills so as not to lose sight of him once they were in the hill country.

Using all their ingenuity and skill the Collins brothers kept their quarry in view as he worked his way through the hills. They were proceeding carefully along a valley which was narrowing rapidly when Jack checked his horse. Howard, who was just behind him, pulled to a halt alongside his brother.

'What's wrong?' asked Howard.

'There's seems to be no way out ahead,'

replied Jack. 'We don't want to ride into a trap, there might be lookouts posted. I reckon we can see where he goes from here.'

Howard looked round. 'I'll git a better view from top of that flat rock,' he said indicating a huge rock which projected from the side of the hill. He threw his reins to his brother and slipped from the saddle. He ran to the base of the rock and was able to climb easily by a succession of boulders to the flat top. He flattened himself on the rock and crept forward to the edge. Evans was still riding along the valley but appeared to be riding more cautiously.

Suddenly Howard gasped and was thankful that his brother had had a hunch about guards. Two men had stepped out from behind a boulder into the path of Evans. Their rifles which they had held at the ready were lowered when they saw the identity of the rider. Howard saw them hold a brief conversation with Evans and then all three looked back along the valley. Collins tensed himself. Had Evans been aware that he was being followed? Suddenly the two men on foot turned behind the boulder and re-appeared with two horses. They climbed into the saddles and the three men put their horses at the steep slope on the left hand side of the valley. Howard breathed more easily; he felt sure their presence was not known to the men ahead. He lay still, watching the men move up the slope until they passed over the sky-line. He scrambled down from the rock and ran back to his brother to whom he reported what he had seen.

'Looks as if Evans has taken the guards with him,' mused Jack thoughtfully. 'We must be near their camp an' I reckon there must be somethin' big in the wind fer him to leave the place unguarded.'

The brothers sent their horses forward slowly along the valley, searching the terrain ahead in case there were any more guards. Satisfied that no one watched them they put their horses up the slope and earth and stones rolled behind them as the horses struggled upwards. Pulling to a halt just below the sky-line Jack swung from the saddle and, whilst he crept forward, Howard held the horses under control. When Jack reached the top of the rise he was surprised to find a narrow ridge, just wide enough for a horse to move slowly along. On the other side the ground dropped steeply to a huge hollow completely encircled by steep sided hills. It was like a grass-filled bowl, and on one side stood three huts, outside of which several men were sitting. To Jack's right the hillside had a more gentle slope and it was on this section that Jack saw the three riders following a zig-zag path to the bottom. When the three men reached the hollow they put their horses into a canter towards the huts.

Jack moved back from the ridge, turned and slithered down the slope to his brother.

'We've found it all right,' he said excitedly, 'but we won't be able to take the horses, we'd better leave them in the valley.'

They mounted and turned the horses down the slope. Reaching the valley amidst a shower of rolling stones and earth the brothers steadied the animals and rode a short distance before securing them in a safe place. Jack and Howard scrambled back up the slope and were soon laid on top of the ridge peering down into the huge bowl.

'That's the only way down,' said Jack pointing to the path, 'so you see why we can't use the horses; we'd be too conspicuous. I reckon we can do it on foot without being seen if we use the boulders as cover.'

Howard nodded then suddenly gripped his brother's arm. 'Looks as if they're leaving,' he said. Several men led horses from one of the huts which must have been used as a stable. There was great activity for a few minutes as the men gathered together, then they mounted their horses and started across the hollow.

'They've got to come out this way,' gasped Jack. He looked round anxiously searching for cover. 'Over there,' he said pointing to a group of low boulders a little below the ridge and some distance to the right.

The two men scrambled quickly across the sloping ground and flattened themselves behind the boulders. They waited tensely and the moments seemed like eternity until the first man appeared on the ridge. The Collins brothers slipped their Colts from their holsters ready for any eventuality. The second rider was Sol Evans and already the first man was turning his horse down the slope to the valley. The brothers watched whilst six men traversed the slope and reached the valley. They gathered together, then rode quickly away.

'Whatever they're on,' said Howard, 'it must be mighty important for Sol to get them moving so quickly. What do we do now, keep following Evans?'

Jack pondered thoughtfully for a moment. 'It looks as if they're bent on another raid.

They hevn't got Lance Peters with them so I reckon he's probably still in that hollow. We've got a good chance to rescue Peters whilst they're away.'

The brothers crept quickly back up the slope and paused to survey the scene.

'Two of them left,' muttered Howard.

'Unless there are any more inside one of the huts,' pointed out Jack.

'I doubt it,' answered Howard. 'We'd better work our way round the edge of the hollow to the right.'

Jack murmured his agreement and the two men crept along the ridge until they reached the downward path. They used every available cover to make their way to the hollow. Reaching the bottom they paused, watching the two men for a moment but neither of them stirred. Jack and Howard hurried as quickly as they dared round the hollow thankful that there was a great deal of cover they could use. Thirty yards from the hut they paused and peered cautiously ahead. There was not an inch of cover for the last thirty yards.

'We can't creep up on them,' whispered Jack, 'we'll hev to take them.'

Howard nodded grimly and both men drew their Colts.

'Right,' whispered Jack. 'Now!'

As one man they stepped from behind the boulder and moved a few paces quickly towards the hut before the two men were startled by the sudden movement.

They dived from their chairs, on which they had been lounging, jerking at their Colts as they did so. The hollow reverberated with the roar of guns and the brothers saw the two men twist as the lead smashed into their bodies. They jerked as if they had hit a wall, then rolled over, their hands still clawing at their guns. They lay still in the grass and Jack and Howard waited, their guns still at the ready. No one else appeared; neither man on the ground moved.

'Cover me,' muttered Jack grimly and started to move slowly towards the men on the ground. When he reached them he stared at them for a moment. 'Dead,' he called over his shoulder and waited for Howard to join him.

The two men walked forward towards the first hut, each covering the other. No sound came from any of the buildings; it seemed that there was no one else in the hollow, but nevertheless Jack and Howard were not prepared to take chances. Jack waved his gun towards the window and Howard moved swiftly to the wall of the hut, pressed himself against it, inched his way to the window and peered cautiously inside. As far as he could see there was no one in the building. He signaled to Jack who had stopped outside the door. Jack kicked at the door which crashed open under the impact. He hesitated a moment then stepped quickly inside. A moment later he appeared.

'No one there,' he called to Howard. 'Let's try this one.'

They moved quickly to the next hut and peered through the window.

'Someone on that bunk,' whispered Howard.

They stepped swiftly but silently to the door and lifted the sneck quietly, and gently tried the door but it was unyielding.

'Must be Peters!' said Jack excitedly.

The two well-built men put their powerful shoulders to the door and with two sharp blows burst it open. The figure on the bed moaned and tried to turn over. The brothers leaped to his side when they saw he was tied hands and feet and gagged. Jack and Howard quickly untied his hands and helped Lance Peters to his feet.

'I'm mighty glad to see you two,' he said rubbing his wrists vigorously to restore the circulation. 'Wondered what all the shooting was about.'

'You all right, Lance,' asked Jack anxiously.

Peters nodded. 'Yes,' he replied. 'But we have no time to lose; the gang's just ridden off to get Mick Hawksley!'

'What!' gasped Jack and Howard.

'I've some other bad news for you,' went on Peters seriously. 'Some hombre rode in here a short while ago with orders from the boss of this outfit. Seems a man called Jamie had followed Dan to Gainesville where he must have found something out because this Jamie had shot him on the way back.'

'No!' Jack and Howard were horrified at the news. They stared at each other in blank amazement.

'Poor Babs,' muttered Howard dejectedly.

'I tried to make a break for it when I heard the news,' explained Lance, 'but I was out of luck and you saw the result.'

'Someone's goin' to answer for this,' hissed Jack angrily. He looked sharply at the other men. 'We can't afford fer anythin' to happen to Lance,' he went on quickly. 'Howard, you take him to the Bar X; he'll be safe with dad; then bring our boys back to Red Springs. I'll head fer town to warn Clint.'

165

The three men ran to the hut used as a stable and were relieved to find three horses. They saddled them quickly and raced across the hollow at full gallop. They urged the animals up the slope and along the ridge as fast as they dare. After getting their own more powerful mounts the grim-faced Collins brothers led the way along the valley at break-neck speed. Once clear of the valley they cut across the hills urging their horses faster. They had travelled about three miles when, with a brief nod, Jack turned his horse away from the others and headed for Red Springs.

He did not spare his horse as he raced from the hills and cut across the undulating grassland. He guessed the gang would take the easy way through the hill country and the better trail to town and he hoped that, by making this rougher but more direct approach he would outride them.

The powerful horse answered his urging and stretched itself in full gallop. When he thundered into the main street he was relieved to see that everything was normal and, as he tore along the street, he yelled to three men who were lounging in chairs outside the saloon. They leaped to their feet, realizing that all was not well, and sprinted after Jack.

When he reached the sheriff's office Jack hauled on the reins bringing the animal to a dust-raising, sliding halt. He was out of the saddle almost before the horse had stopped. Leaping on to the sidewalk he burst into the office startling Clint Schofield with the suddenness of his appearance.

'There's a raid comin',' he panted. 'Dan's been killed an' the masked gang are headin' fer town to git Mick.'

Clint stared unbelievingly at Jack at the news of Dan's death. He was shaken out of his shock and galvanized into action when the three men ran into the office. As he handed out rifles Jack told him all the details.

'I reckon we'll sit tight in here,' Clint said grimly when Jack had finished, 'an' hold them off until Howard arrives with help.' He crossed to the door and locked and bolted it. 'They'll sure be surprised when we're ready for them.' His eyes narrowed. 'An' everyone of them will answer fer what's happened to Dan!'

Chapter Ten

Sol Evans kept the gang to a steady pace for he knew that to push the horses too hard now might prove disastrous later. They would require their energy after the raid when there might be a lot of hard, fast riding to do. He grinned to himself; things had gone well and before long he figured he would be sharing much of the Twisted M and Broken K spreads.

They required the all clear from Jamie whom the boss had sent back to Red Springs after he had reported the shooting of Dan McCoy. With the element of surprise in their favour they would soon have Mick Hawksley at the end of a rope.

About a mile out of town Sol pulled off the trail and rode to an outcrop of huge rocks where the gang dismounted and kept out of sight whilst one man climbed a rock to keep a look out in the direction of Red Springs. Twenty minutes passed before he sighted a lone rider and once he recognized him he scrambled down from his vantage point.

'He's comin',' he told Evans.

The men checked their guns and awaited the arrival of Jamie.

'How's things?' asked Sol.

'Couldn't be better,' answered Jamie with a grin as he swung off his horse. 'There's only the old deputy at the jail; the Collins brothers aren't around an' there are very few folks in town.'

'Good,' grinned Sol. 'This is going to be easy.' He looked round the men. 'Everyone ready?' They all nodded. 'Right,' went on Evans, 'we'll wear masks from here on in. You all know the plan when we reach town and after we've got Hawksley you head fer the Twisted M. The boss an' I will bring the others there an' then we'll hev a nice little party.'

The men grinned as they pulled their neckerchiefs up over the lower half of their faces. They climbed into the saddles and with Sol in the lead headed for Red Springs.

They quickened their pace as they neared the town and with no attempt to hide their presence they thundered into the main street. The party split; two men moved to the right hand side of the street and pulled to a halt half way between the edge of town and the sheriff's office whilst two more did the same on the other side. One man rode quickly up a side street to approach the jail from the back and Sol and Jamie headed straight for the sheriff's office. There were only four people on the street and as soon as they saw the masked riders they ran for cover not wanting to be involved in any trouble. A man stepped out of the saloon but a warning shot by one of the gang sent him scurrying back.

Sol and Jamie were rapidly approaching the sheriff's office when suddenly a rifle crashed and a bullet whined unpleasantly close to Jamie's head. Both men, shaken by this unexpected reception hauled on the reins, and turned their horses away from the firing which had now burst from the sheriff's office. Masked men dived from their horses and Sol and Jamie flung themselves behind a water trough.

'They're on us,' snarled Sol. 'How did they know?'

'Somethin' must hev happened after I left,' replied Jamie. 'There was only old Schofield at the jail then. Sure no one saw you?'

Sol's answer was left unspoken. Instead he cursed loudly as a bullet spanged into the trough sending a shower of water on to him.

As Clint Schofield watched the gang ride

into Red Springs he told the four men at the windows to hold their fire until the last moment but unfortunately one of the men was a little too eager and his shot acted as a warning. Clint cursed under his breath but the damage was done and already the gang were seeking cover. He yelled to everyone to fire but the two horsemen seemed to bear a charmed life and they had dived behind a water trough almost before the men in the office realized it.

An answering fusillade of shots crashed into the building and the men ducked back from the windows. The firing became spasmodic but every time the men in the building were driven back from the windows they knew the gang were closing a little nearer the jail.

'We've got to hold them off until Howard gits here,' said Jack. 'He shouldn't be long now; I reckon he'd reach the Bar X about the same time as I got here.'

He loosed off a couple of shots through the window and then ducked out of sight. One man who had done the same was not quick enough and a bullet crashed into his right shoulder sending him reeling backwards. Clint jumped to his side and a quick glance told him that the wound was a bad one. Jack looked anxiously at Clint as the deputy tried to staunch the flow of blood. He dropped to his knees as shots whined into the building, and crawled to Clint's side.

'This is no good,' he said desperately. 'They know where they've got us but with them altering their positions we're just firing blind. I'm goin' out of the back door, lock it again after me, Clint.'

'You're not to go,' rapped Clint. 'It would be suicide for you to be alone out there.'

'Not if they don't know I've gone outside,' said Jack. 'We've got to hev another gun in a different place,' insisted Jack and before Clint could reply he jumped to his feet and hurried to the back door. Clint leaped after him and, not wishing to argue with the deputy, Jack flung open the door and stepped outside. His haste was almost his undoing. A Colt roared and a bullet clipped Jack's ear and buried itself in the wooden wall of the building. A masked man who had been creeping towards the back door had been so surprised when Jack appeared suddenly that his aim had not been true. The Colt roared again but Jack had acted instinctively to the first shot and was already diving into the dust. He rolled over finishing up on his stomach with his Colt held ready for action. The masked man crouched, swinging his Colt for a third shot but Jack's gun crashed, sending lead into the man's stomach. The man doubled up grasping at his body with his free hand. His finger squeezed the trigger again but already his knees were buckling and the bullet buried itself harmlessly in the ground. Jack fired again and the masked man pitched to the ground where he lay still in a huddled heap. Jack remained where he was for a few moments watching the man carefully before he started to climb to his feet. Clint, who had been startled by the suddenness of the action, rushed outside.

'Git back to the front,' called Jack, 'an' keep them busy, I'm all right.' He set off down the alley without waiting for Clint's reply and the deputy sheriff knew it was useless to try to stop him. He stepped back into the jail, relocked the door and called to the two able men to keep up a rapid fire to hold the attention of the raiders.

Jack ran along the alley, pausing at the end of the block. He glanced round the corner towards Main Street and seeing no one, sprinted across the gap to the opposite building which had a flat roof. He holstered his Colt and hurried to a water tub a few yards along the alley. Turning it upside down he climbed on to it, jumped upwards and with outstretched arms grasped the edge of the roof. Pulling himself up he scrambled on to the top of the building. Jack took his gun from the holster and crept across the roof to the low parapet which stretched the width of the building. He took off his Stetson and raised his head to see two men shielded by crates were firing at the sheriff's office. A rifle crashed below him and he knew that there was at least one man on this side of the street. Two more shots barked from further along the street but Jack could not detect the exact position from which they had come.

He raised his gun and, taking careful aim, squeezed the trigger gently. One of the men opposite jerked as the bullet found its mark and he pitched forward against the crates sending them crashing on to the boardwalk. The second man, startled by the unexpected attack, twisted round and dived into a doorway as Jack's Colt roared again. The bullet nicked his arm but it was only a flesh wound and in terror he blazed away at the roof on which Jack was already scrambling quickly to the rear of the building. He swung over the edge of the building lowering himself to the full extent of his arms then dropped to the ground. He raced further along the alley, turned into a side street and ran towards Main Street. Stopping at the corner he peered cautiously round but a bullet split the woodwork close to his head and he jerked back cursing the man who had been so keen eyed as to detect the movement.

He hesitated, formulating his next move when he heard a yell and the thunder of hoofs at the far end of town. Guns roared and feet pounded on the sidewalk. Two horses flashed past the end of the street, masked men crouching low on their backs. Without fear of the possible consequences Jack stepped out of the side street. Two men were racing along the sidewalk and were on top of him before any of them realized it. They sent him sprawling into the dust under the impact but, managing to keep their own balance, they ran on, leaped on to their horses and followed their two companions in an earth-shaking gallop. Jack started to scramble to his feet when he saw the man whom he had wounded leap from the doorway to his horse. Jack stopped in the kneeling position and raised his Colt. He squeezed the trigger and saw the man jerk as the horse broke into a gallop. He slumped forward round the frightened animal's neck and then slid slowly off its back. Jack stared, horrified as the man hit the ground one foot still fastened in the stirrup. He bounced and bumped through the dust as the horse tore onwards dragging him behind. It was only at the end of the street that his foot became loose but the horse raced onwards leaving the man rolling over and over until his battered body came to a stop against a small mound of earth. Jack knew without further investigation that the man would be dead.

He was jerked out of his trance by the thunder of hoofs and he looked up to see Howard who was leading the Bar X cowboys already starting to pull up.

'Get after them,' yelled Jack. 'Sol Evans was amongst them an' we want him.' He noted the look of concern on his brother's face. 'We're all right,' he shouted.

Howard pushed his horse back into a gallop and with the Bar X cowboys close behind him thundered out of Red Springs along the north road.

Jack hurried towards the sheriff's office and as he neared it a man stepped out and ran quickly in the direction of Doc Smith's. 'Any more casualties?' asked Jack when he entered the office.

'No,' answered Clint. 'Mart's badly hurt but Jim's gone for Doc Smith. Hope Howard catches those hombres.'

'Sol Evans is the one I want,' said Jack grimly. 'I'll make him talk!'

'Thet'll be my pleasure after what's happened to Dan,' muttered Clint between tight lips.

A few moments later Doc Smith hurried in, quickly attended to the wounded man announcing that he would be all right in a fortnight if he took things easy. He told the other two men to take him home and after they had gone Clint and Jack settled down to await the return of Howard. After about five minutes Jack began to grow restless and started to pace up and down. Clint brewed some coffee and poured out three mugs full taking one to Mick Hawksley who, during the raid, had pleaded to be let out of the cell and given a gun, but it was something the lawman dare not risk.

Jack walked up and down nervously flexing his fingers, anxious for Howard, hoping for Sol Evans in order to make him talk and clear this thing up quickly. He wanted the man called Jamie and more than that he wanted the leader of this gang but even then would he have the killer of Kathy? As far as he could see they were still as far from that as ever; according to Lance Peters Dan had found something out in Gainesville but Dan was dead.

Half an hour passed and Jack walked to the window, once again looking along the north road hoping to see Howard returning with some prisoners. As he turned from the window his gaze passed along the street in the opposite direction. He froze in his tracks, staring incredulously, hardly able to believe his eyes. A lone rider, his left arm in a sling, rode slowly along the street, and already a few people were hurrying towards him.

'Dan!' whispered Jack to himself then suddenly he leaped for the door. 'Dan's alive!' he yelled. 'Dan's here.'

Clint jumped from his chair knocking it over in his excitement. Jack tore open the door and the two men raced outside as Dan pulled to a halt. Clint jumped off the sidewalk and held Dan's horse as Jack helped the wounded man out of the saddle.

'Mighty glad to see you're all right, Dan,' called someone in the small crowd which had gathered.

Dan smiled and helped by his friends entered his office.

'Thought you were dead,' said Jack.

'Takes a lot to kill me,' grinned Dan. 'An' don't fuss so, I'm all right, just a bit weak. But how did you hear I was dead?'

Jack and Clint related the events since Dan had ridden to Gainesville and he listened thoughtfully without interruption. He pursed his lips and rubbed his chin looking at Jack when he had finished his story.

'Evans is the link man,' he said, 'but he met no one in the hollow that first night and he rode off to contact the gang the following afternoon. You say that Rockhill appeared to give him orders.' He paused, a puzzled look on his face. 'If this gang an' Kathy's murder are connected that doesn't fit in with what I learned in Gainesville.'

'What about Evans himself; could he be the boss?' put in Clint.

'Lance Peters said he overheard Evans say he'd come from the boss,' pointed out Jack.

'You're sure no one else contacted Evans?' asked Dan.

Jack nodded. 'Certain.'

'Let's go over what happened at the Twisted M from the time Rockhill left,' suggested Dan.

'Evans went to the corral and started work on some horses,' related Jack. 'At noon he stopped for a meal; had it with two other

Twisted M hands who had been repairing fences; then he returned to his horses and was with them until he rode off.'

'He spoke to no one else?' asked a puzzled Dan.

'Wal, Burt Weldon of the Broken K was ridin' past. He stopped fer a while watching Evans. Evans was havin' a rough time with one of the horses an' Weldon went over and helped him, he sure can handle a horse but he was...'

'That's it,' yelled Dan cutting in. Both men stared at the excited sheriff. 'It fits in, shaggy eyebrows; can handle horses. We're on to him but we'll hev to work fast so I'll put you in the picture later. If he gits word this raid failed he may try to ride out but he thinks I'm dead so he may stay, however we can't take chances. Jack, git to the Broken K as fast as possible, look out fer anyone trying to contact Weldon and what is more important don't let anyone leave the ranch. Keep them there at the point of the gun if necessary. Clint, you ride to the Bar X and bring Lance Peters back here then we'll all take Mick home.'

The two men hurried from the office and as Dan heard their horses pounding along the street he started to sort things out in his mind.

Chapter Eleven

As Sol Evans thundered away from Red Springs he cursed his luck wondering how the lawman knew of their intentions. His thoughts raced and he saw that the plans, made two years ago and put into operation when his boss seized the opportunity ten days ago after he had followed Kathy into town, crumbling about them. But was everything lost? The identity of his boss was not known and if he could warn him what had happened he might have fresh ideas.

Sol glanced at Jamie racing alongside him. 'Cut off at the fork,' he yelled, 'head for the hills.'

Jamie nodded and urged his horse faster. The other two members of the gang were close behind and when they reached the fork in the trail they followed Jamie along the left hand trail as Sol broke away to the right.

The Bar X cowboys led by Howard Collins were not far behind and Howard waved them after the three men as he guided his horse to the right. Evans glanced over his shoulder anxiously and was somewhat relieved to see only one man pursuing him but when he recognized Howard Collins he knew he would have a hard job to shake him off. He urged his horse faster and the powerful animal answered his call. Hoofs flashed across the ground and the gap between Evans and Collins was gradually widening.

When Howard saw Evans moving further away he cursed himself for not getting a fresh mount at the Bar X but he had been anxious to get back to Red Springs. His horse had been ridden hard for a great part of the day and the fresher animal ahead was pulling away from him. Howard urged his horse but it was at full stretch and although he realized he would not catch Sol Evans he stuck doggedly to the pursuit.

Evans was well ahead of Collins when the trail dropped into a narrow gully through which flowed a stream. When he reached the ford he turned his horse up the stream towards the narrow end of the gully where it gradually rose to the grassland. He reached a clump of small trees and halted his horse waiting anxiously for Howard to appear and hoping that he had anticipated correctly Howard's actions when he realized Evans was no long ahead of him.

Howard reached the gully at full gallop, he flashed down the slope, splashed through the ford and tore up the other side. It was some moments before he realized that Evans had given him the slip. 'Must hev turned in the gully,' he muttered to himself as he pulled his horse to a halt. He swung the animal round and rode quickly back to the gully. Pausing on the edge of the slope he looked around but could see no sign of the man he was pursuing. He rode down the slope and halted in the water. He glanced up the gully little realizing that a Colt covered him, ready should he move in that direction. 'With the lead he had he'd be a fool to go up that way,' muttered Howard. 'He must have gone down-stream.' He turned his horse and rode through the water.

Sol Evans holstered his gun grinning to himself. He had been right. Waiting until Howard was well out of sight he turned his horse up the steep slope on to the grassland and headed for the Broken K ranch.

Howard moved cautiously down the stream his eyes searching every available cover for some sight of Evans. He reckoned that Evans would keep to the water to hide his tracks but nevertheless he watched the banks of the stream in case Evans had taken another route. It was only after about twenty minutes that Howard began to have doubts and finally he came to the conclusion that Evans had given him the slip. Annoyed with himself he reluctantly decided that the only thing he could do was to return to Red Springs. He turned out of the gully and rode across the grassland in the direction of town.

He came on to the trail close to the fork and his annoyance was somewhat appeased by the sight of the Bar X cowboys approaching with their prisoners. He waited until they reached him.

'You've had better luck than me,' he said. 'Evans gave me the slip.'

'They gave us a hard ride,' explained the foreman, 'and when they realized we were overhauling them they made a bit of a stand in a hollow. We were too many for them and they soon knew that.'

'Then there's only Evans and the boss still free,' said Howard as the party turned their horses towards town.

They had ridden about a quarter of a mile when they saw a dust-cloud rising ahead and observed a posse of horsemen riding quickly towards them. Howard halted his party watching the approaching men carefully. Suddenly he yelled with relief and a smile crossed his face when he recognized Dan McCoy in the lead. He kicked his horse forward and galloped to meet them.

'Mighty glad to see you, Dan,' he said as they all pulled to a halt.'

'Did you git Evans?' asked Clint anxiously.

Howard shook his head glumly. 'Gave me the slip after he'd split from the others but the boys got them.'

'Good,' said Dan, 'they can take them back to town; you come with us. Clint, cut off at the fork an' bring Rockhill to the Broken K.'

Howard nodded and they were about to send their horses forward when Dan halted the prisoners. He stared hard at Jamie.

'I've seen you somewhere before,' he said but the man did not answer. 'Got it!' snapped Dan suddenly. 'You were in Gainesville, next to me in the saloon. It must hev been you who shot me.' He nodded to the Bar X cowboys and they set off for Red Springs with the prisoners.

'What goes on?' asked Howard for apart from seeing Dan he had been surprised to see Mick Hawksley and Lance Peters.

'No time for explanations,' replied Dan. 'Let's hope Jack got to the Broken K quickly; Evans may try to git there.'

The four men pushed their horses forward at a fast pace for the Broken K whilst Clint headed for the Twisted M.

Jack Collins did not spare his horse when he left Red Springs for the Broken K. He had been overjoyed to see Dan and, realizing that his brother-in-law was near solving the present troubles, he knew the urgency of his mission. With Peter Hawksley's herd still a day's ride away Jack knew that the only people at the ranch were Pete Hawksley, his wife, Jim Masters and Burt Weldon. It would be easy to see that none of them left the ranch if they were all still there. The more difficult part of his task was to see that no one watched or contacted Weldon and as he galloped northwards Jack formulated a plan.

About half a mile from the Broken K he eased his pace and worked his way round to a group of boulders from which he could watch the ranch. Slipping from his horse's back he surveyed the ranch and was thankful to see Burt Weldon working with Pete Hawksley and Jim Masters close to the stables. He was about to return to his horse and ride to the house when he noted a lone rider emerge from the hollow to the right and head for the group of boulders. Jack looked round, he did not want to be seen and he reckoned with any luck he could remain hidden even if the man stopped close by.

Jack led his horse into a narrow cutting between two huge rocks, then positioned himself so that he could watch the man. Suddenly he stiffened – it was Sol Evans! So he had managed to get away from Howard. Jack drew his Colt and watched Evans nearing the upheaval of boulders. When he reached them he stopped, swung from the saddle, climbed to an advantageous position and surveyed the ranch through a spy-glass.

He lay there a few minutes then, much to Jack's surprise, he climbed to his feet and stood upon the rock. Jack glanced towards the Broken K. The three men were still working. He saw Burt Weldon straighten and as he turned, which brought him facing the direction of the boulders, he noticed him pause before resuming work. Jack looked back at Evans who swung round and started to scramble down from the rock. Suddenly Jack realized that Evans could not ride up to the ranch to contact Weldon but by revealing himself from this distance he knew Weldon would ride out to meet him.

Knowing he must act quickly Jack crept swiftly but quietly round two huge boulders and stepped into the open just as Evans reached his horse.

'Hold it, Evans!' snapped Jack.

Evans, surprised by the unexpected and sudden command, spun round. His face lost its colour when he saw the cold muzzle of a Colt covering him from the hand of Jack Collins. He crouched like some cornered animal his eyes darting here and there seeking some means of escape.

'Don't try anythin',' warned Jack. 'The game's up and you aren't warning Weldon.' He noted with satisfaction the startled look on Evans' face at the mention of Weldon's name.

Jack moved forward intending to disarm the man but, so intent was he on watching Evans, that he failed to notice the hole in front of him. He caught his foot and stumbled. For a moment his aim was thrown off Evans and the man seized his chance. He drew his Colt in a flash but Jack regained his balance and as Evans squeezed the trigger Jack's Colt roared. Jack felt the bullet rip through his shirt sleeve and nick his arm but he saw Evans stagger under the blow which he received under the heart. Jack fired again and the man crashed back against a boulder and slid to the ground, to lie still.

Jack knew he had not a moment to lose. The shots must have been heard by the men at the ranch and he reckoned that Weldon must be wondering what had caused the firing when only a few moments ago he had seen Evans standing on the rock. Jack could not afford to waste a minute in case Weldon tried to leave the ranch. He raced to his horse and was soon galloping towards the Broken K.

As he came from behind the boulders he saw Masters and Weldon running to the stable and Hawksley entering the ranch-house. He urged his horse faster and was close to the house when Hawksley re-appeared and his two men emerged from the stable leading three horses. Hawksley, a look of surprise on his face when he saw Jack Collins galloping towards the house, stopped on the verandah. Jack was out of the saddle before his horse had stopped and leaped on to the verandah beside Hawksley.

'Howdy, Jack,' greeted the rancher. 'What happened over there?' He nodded in the direction of the boulders.

'Everything's all right,' panted Jack. 'Don't worry. Tell your men to put the horses back then get them into the house.'

Hawksley looked startled at this request but he did not query it as Masters and Weldon were close by. 'It's all right,' he said to them. 'You can put the horses back we don't need them, it was only Jack over there.'

Masters and Weldon looked questioningly at the two men on the verandah but when no further explanation was forthcoming they returned to the stable.

When they passed out of sight Hawksley turned to Jack. 'What's this all about?' he demanded.

'There's no time fer explanations,' replied Jack, 'Dan will be here shortly and he'll give you all the answers. Jest git them into the house then I can keep an eye on you all and see no one leaves.'

'What!' There was a note of annoyance in Hawksley's voice. 'Anyone can leave this ranch as and when they please. I'll not...'

'If you want Mick's name clearing do as I ask,' broke in Jack.

There was a note of urgency in Jack's voice which made Hawksley realize he had to do as he was asked. He turned to the door of the house and stepped inside calling to his wife. A moment later he reappeared and when the two men came out of the stable he called them over.

'We'll leave the work for the day,' he said. 'It will soon be dark anyhow. Mrs Hawksley has a meal ready so you'd both better come in an' share it. Jack, will you join us?'

The three men muttered their thanks and followed Pete Hawksley into the house. Jack was thankful for Hawksley's quick thinking in offering this invitation to his two men; it was going to make things easier. He hoped that Dan would arrive before the meal was over otherwise he might have to use a gun to make them stay. He wanted to avoid that if possible for he knew it could lead to an awkward situation but he was prepared to use force should the necessity arise. Mrs Hawksley was rather slow in bringing the meal to the table saying that it was not quite ready and Jack realized that when Pete had gone to the kitchen to tell his wife they were ready he must have tipped her off to delay things. Jack made a mental note to thank him when this was all over.

Throughout the meal Hawksley kept a conversation going about ranch affairs and the herd which he was expecting. All the time Jack strained his ears to catch the sound of approaching horses but they had finished the meal and still he heard nothing.

Burt Weldon and Jim Masters were pushing themselves to their feet and thanking Mrs Hawksley when he caught the distant clop of hoofs. He tensed himself ready to take action but once again Hawksley, who had also heard the riders, acted quickly.

'Just wait a minute both of you,' he said. 'I hev a bonus I'd like to pay you for the way you've worked with those horses these last few days.' He turned to his desk then paused, listening. 'More visitors,' he said. 'Hold on an' I'll see who it is first.'

Jack relaxed, relieved of the necessity for drastic action. Hawksley hurried outside.

He gasped when he saw his son was one of the four riders pulling to a halt in front of the house. They swung from the saddle and stepped on to the verandah.

'Mick!' gasped Hawksley gripping his son's arm. 'Is he free?' he asked, turning to Dan.

Dan smiled. 'Not yet, Pete. Is Jack Collins here?'

'Inside,' replied Pete and indicated to the newcomers to enter the house.

'Well done, Jack,' said Dan when he entered the room.

'I think we have Pete to thank really,' said Jack with a grin at the rancher.

'Mick!' cried Mrs Hawksley when she saw

her son. She rushed forward flinging her arms around him. 'You're free!' Her tear-filled eyes looked up at him.

'Not yet, mother,' replied Mick. 'But don't worry,' he added seeing disappointment cross her face. 'This is Lance Peters who's goin' to defend me.'

Lance shook hands with Mr and Mrs Hawksley.

'I'm mighty glad you're all right,' said Pete. 'I hope you weren't badly handled by your kidnappers.'

'No,' replied Lance, 'and I have to thank the Collins boys for rescuing me.'

Dan was watching Burt Weldon carefully but the man's face remained impassive although Dan knew his brain must be in a turmoil at seeing him bring in Lance Peters and Mick Hawksley.

His thoughts were interrupted when he heard Pete Hawksley asking him what was the matter with his arm. 'Someone tried to kill me on my way back from Gainesville,' he explained, 'but we got the would-be killer.' He continued to watch Weldon closely when he asked Jack if he'd seen anything of Evans.

'Had to kill him when he tried to get me, close to the Broken K,' replied Jack.

Dan thought he detected a faint look of

startled surprise in Weldon's eyes but he had to admire the way the man remained calm.

'I guess we'd better be goin',' said Jim Masters. 'Thanks once again for the meal.'

'I'd like you both to wait,' said Dan coolly with an authoritative note in his voice.

Jim Masters looked surprised but nodded. He respected the law especially as upheld by the Sheriff of Red Springs. Burt Weldon's face was blank. He shrugged his shoulders and moved close to one of the windows. He had been astonished when the sheriff had walked in with Lance Peters. He had thought McCoy was dead and Peters still a prisoner in the hills. Something had gone wrong somewhere and he realized with the capture of Jamie, the killing of Evans and the information gained in Gainesville that the sheriff was on to something and that his plans had been forestalled. But did the sheriff connect him with the story he'd heard in Gainesville and with Kathy's murder? Whatever happened Weldon swore to himself that he would see the conclusion of some of his plans even though he would not see the fruition of them all.

'What's all this about?' Pete Hawksley asked Dan.

'All in good time,' came the reply. 'There

are two other people to come yet; they shouldn't be long.'

There was an uneasy tenseness in the room as the nine people waited. Some of them tried to start conversations but no one seemed to want to talk. Everyone wished the sound of horses' hoofs would put an end to the tension. In spite of the fact that they were all listening intently everyone seemed to be surprised when they heard the approaching animals. Howard, who had been standing close to the door as if on guard, hurried through the hallway to the outside door. The others, with the exception of Dan, who kept his eye on Weldon, faced the door, a mixture of curiosity and expectancy on their faces.

The horses stopped and feet clattered on the verandah. Al Rockhill, his frame filling the doorway, stepped into the room. He paused, surprised to see so many people there then he spotted Mick Hawksley.

'What's that little runt doin' here again?' he demanded harshly, his face darkening with anger. 'What's this all about, McCoy?'

'Now you've arrived everyone will find out,' replied Dan coldly. He moved to one side so that he faced everyone in the room. 'When Kathy Rockhill was murdered I had no option but to arrest Mick Hawksley but something made me search further. I had to make sure he was the killer. I found traces of clay in Mick's hotel; clay which could only have come from a certain part of the Broken K ranch and yet Mick had not been out here for a couple of days. Immediately after the murder a masked gang appeared in the hills and both Twisted M and Broken K were hit. There was nothing to connect the masked gang with Kathy's murder and after I realized that it could not be either Hawksley or Rockhill seeking revenge upon each other I figured that may be this gang was seeking revenge upon them both.' Dan paused and everyone hung expectantly on his words. 'I had to try to find a common denominator, someone who wished harm to them both. Pete I've known a long time but Al only for the past five years. He was to some extent unknown to me so I tried to probe his past. This resulted in my visit to Gainesville where I heard a very interesting story.'

Rockhill was startled by this news. 'See here, McCoy, you've no right...'

'I have every right, Al,' cut in Dan, 'and you'd better let me finish. Sufficient for me to say that a certain Al Richards made an enemy in Gainesville. Life was beginning to become unpleasant for him and his daughter and when this enemy tried to kill them they left the area and sought out a new home. Pete Hawksley was kind to Al Richards and his daughter Kathy.'

Pete looked hard at Al. 'You were this Richards?' he asked.

Al nodded. 'I tried to lose myself under another name. You see at his trial this man swore to get both Kathy and myself. I succeeded only to have Kathy killed by another.'

'Not another,' said Dan coolly but firmly. Rockhill looked at him disbelievingly. 'Al Richards, I want you to meet Ben Wilson,' he added, indicating Burt Weldon.

Rockhill stared at Weldon. 'You're mistaken,' he said slowly. Weldon did not move nor say a word.

'I don't think so,' said Dan. 'Ben Wilson served a prison sentence which went hard with him, he was so eaten up with hate that it left its mark firmly upon him and it was in this change that he saw his means of being close to you without the chance of recognition. Two characteristics he forgot to get rid of – shaggy eyebrows, the other, his outstanding ability to handle horses. Burt Weldon fits both those accounts.'

Rockhill, doubting Weldon's identity, started forward towards him but Dan stopped him. Weldon looked coldly at the sheriff.

'You cannot accuse a man on shaggy eyebrows and love of horses,' he said quietly.

Dan admired the coolness of the man. Could he not be shaken? He ignored Weldon's remark and continued. 'Ben Wilson returned to Gainesville on his release from jail but he found Richards had gone. He was determined to find him and when he left some of the good-for-nothings of the town went with him.' Dan paused; from here on a lot of what he would say would be guesswork but Dan had given it a lot of thought whilst waiting for Clint to bring Lance Peters from the Bar X and he reckoned he would not be far off the mark. 'Ben Wilson eventually found out that Richards had settled near Red Springs. He and his little gang hid out in the hills. He was prepared to await the right opportunity for his revenge and I believe he had thought about it so much in jail that he wanted to take things slowly – enjoying it as you might say. He daren't move too near the Twisted M for, in spite of the fact that he had altered, there might be something which Kathy or her father might recognize if he was seen by them often. He obtained a job with Pete here and one of his men, Sol Evans, got work at the Twisted M. They had a pre-arranged meeting place half way between the two ranches and so he was able to keep a close watch on Richards and at the same time be in contact with his gang.'

Dan saw Weldon's jaw tightening and the muscles in his face twitch nervously. His eyes were smouldering with anger and hate and Dan knew that his suppositions were near the mark.

'I reckon that it was about this time that Ben Wilson conceived the idea of playing a bigger game and that, apart from the killing of Richards and his daughter, he would take over their ranch.'

'All right, Mister Clever Sheriff.' The words spat across the room and it was only then that everyone realized they had been so intent on Dan's story that they had not noticed Weldon's hand moving towards his Colt and Dan himself had dropped his vigilance for a second. Weldon seized the opportunity and his Colt leaped into his hand. 'You're right, I'm Ben Wilson. I came for revenge as you said but one thing you don't know, I loved Kathy. I was even pre-pared to forget the way she snubbed mc in Gainesville and hoped that maybe there was still a chance fer me with her. That, more than anything, stopped me from killing Richards as soon as I found him. I was prepared to wait but then after some time I learned she loved Mick Hawksley. It was then I got bigger ideas, not just the Twisted M, McCoy, but the Broken K as well. I'd kill Richards for what he did to my parents, Kathy for snubbing me and Hawksley fer lovin' her.' He paused for breath, a fire of excitement had come into his eyes. 'You may as well have the lot. I began following Kathy and when she went after Mick into Red Springs I overheard her tell the hotel clerk she was goin' to marry Mick. When he got drunk the chance of killin' Kathy, planting the murder on Mick and playin' Rockhill off against Hawksley was too good to miss.' He edged nearer the window. Dan watched him carefully knowing that at any moment that Colt would speak death.

'I won't finish up with the two spreads now but of one thing I'm certain I'll hev revenge on you, Richards, fer what you did five years ago.'

His finger began to squeeze slowly on the trigger. Dan flung himself sideways with all his force against the huge frame of Rockhill. He sent the rancher staggering as the roar of

Weldon's Colt filled the room. The bullet whined unpleasantly close to Dan's head as he and Rockhill fell to the floor.

At the same moment as he fired Weldon threw himself at the window and, with a loud splintering of glass, crashed to the ground outside. He rolled over, jumped to his feet and ran for the corner of the building.

In spite of having one arm in a sling Dan was on his feet in a flash and, throwing caution to the winds, leaped through the window after Weldon. He jerked his Colt from its holster and as Weldon reached the corner of the house he fired. The bullet took Weldon high on the back of the shoulder. He staggered and spun round, his face black with fury as he faced the sheriff.

Dan moved forward slowly, his eyes on Weldon. 'Drop that gun,' he ordered coldly.

Weldon backed slowly as Dan drew nearer. Reaching the end of the building Weldon suddenly threw himself sideways seeking protection round the corner. Dan anticipated the move and leaped forward flinging himself as far as he could. As he hit the hard ground a searing pain tore at his wounded shoulder but he rolled over which brought him level with the end of the house. Dan's action had been so swift that Weldon was taken completely by surprise and before he realized it Dan had twisted over bringing his Colt to bear on Weldon. Dan squeezed the trigger and, even as Weldon brought his Colt round, the lead crashed into his chest. Weldon's finger closed round the trigger as his head dropped and his knees started to buckle. The shot shattered the ground at his feet and he pitched forward into the dust to lie still.

Feet pounded up as Dan started to push himself from the ground. Jack and Howard helped him to his feet as the others ran up. Rockhill stopped then turned and looked at the dead man before turning to walk slowly to the house. The others followed and when they entered the building he looked at both Mick and his father.

'I'm sorry,' he said hoarsely. 'I hope you'll forgive me.'

Pete smiled and extended his hand which Rockhill took gratefully in a firm grip.

Mick looked at Dan. 'Thanks for all you've done,' he said, 'especially for believing in my innocence. There is something which you should know, Mister Rockhill,' he went on, 'and mother and dad are in for a surprise as well. When Kathy came to Red Springs that night we had a bit of a row; you see, like a lot more people she assumed I was going to marry her. Oh, I liked her a lot an' maybe things would hev turned out all right if I hadn't met a girl in Quanah. I wanted to prove my capabilities to dad and helped this girl, whose father and mother had been killed in a buggy accident, to run her ranch. I fell in love with her and now I want to marry her.'

Pete Hawksley and his wife, taken aback at first, were pleased with the news but before they could speak Al Rockhill stepped forward.

'Congratulations, Mick,' he said extending his hand. 'I guess some of us were too presumptuous about you an' Kathy.' He paused thoughtfully. 'You say this girl is alone, well so am I; bring her over some time, maybe she'll be a worthwhile successor for the Twisted M.'

Rockhill turned and walked from the house before anyone realized the full significance of his words.